The Things I Would Tell You

The Things I Would Tell You

British Muslim Women Write

Edited by Sabrina Mahfouz

SAQI

Published 2017 by Saqi Books

ISBN 978-0-86356-146-7
eISBN 978-0-86356-151-1

A full CIP record for this book is available from the British Library.

Printed by Bell & Bain Limited, Glasgow, G46 7UQ.

Saqi Books
26 Westbourne Grove
London W2 5RH
www.saqibooks.com

Supported using public funding by

ARTS COUNCIL
ENGLAND

Contents

Sabrina Mahfouz

Introduction

I felt upset and angered by the misrepresentations I encountered constantly and I felt grateful when a clear-eyed truth was spoken about us. And then again, who was 'us'?

And so the question is asked by Ahdaf Soueif in *Mezzaterra* in relation to being a Muslim living in the West – who was 'us'? It is a question that has prompted the creation of the book you hold in your hands. At the time of writing, this question is one that a person of Muslim heritage living in the West cannot possibly ignore, even if they hadn't previously given it much thought. Our media is deluged by stories about Muslim extremists; Muslim moderates condemning the actions of Muslim extremists; non-Muslims bemoaning the fact that not enough moderate Muslims are condemning the actions of extremist Muslims; the possibilities of your Muslim-next-door becoming radicalised, perhaps even at their local primary school. This coverage has now been compounded by post-Brexit reports of a catastrophic rise in Islamophobic attacks across Britain, the majority of which have been targeted at women. The monitoring group on anti-Muslim attacks, Tell MAMA, states on its website that the rise in Islamophobic assaults reported to it in 2015 was already up 326 per cent, with the majority of perpetrators being young white males. There has also been a significant increase in hate crimes on public transport and social media, which many analysts view as unprecedented.

In some areas of the country, including London, women who wear Islamic clothing have reported being unable to leave the house for fear of abuse. 'Islamic clothing' could cover anything from a loose-fitting headscarf to a niqab (veil covering all of the face apart from the eyes) or an abaya (full-length, sleeveless outer garment). As one of the many thousands of women in this country with both a Muslim heritage and an aesthetic that can be easily assimilated into a European identity, who chooses to wear clothing that is not explicitly Islamic (though I do usually wear a head covering of sorts, as do many from other cultures), I am in the privileged position of not being a target for these attacks based on appearance.

In the face of such genuine cause for fear, it seems difficult to employ the arts in a truly effective and empowering way. However, one of the aims of this anthology is to dispel the narrow image of what a Muslim woman – particularly a British Muslim woman – looks and lives like. All of the contributors in this book identify as having both a British and a Muslim background or association, regardless of their birthplace, citizenship status or religiosity. The writers were born in or have parentage from countries including France, Iraq, Pakistan, India, Egypt, Lebanon, Jordan, Palestine, Sudan, Somalia and Iran and yet they live, love, create and work in Britain.

Some of the writers featured in this anthology have made public proclamations about the importance of Islam in all aspects of their life; some are passionately secular; and others relate to Islam purely in terms of a cultural tradition that they have inherited. If we can offer an alternative to the current homogenous narrative of British Muslim identity – an alternative that is broadly representative rather than fabricated for political purposes – real change could be made in the lives of those who, as in Chimene Suleyman's powerful story, *Us*, may be shouted at in the street, made to feel paralysed, threatened, unwelcome and, most heart-breakingly, scared for their loved ones in the very place they were born, live or work.

As gloomy as all this is, the words in the forthcoming pages are threaded together by a glow of strength, solidarity, possibility and hope. In Kamila Shamsie's funny and sparkling short story *The Girl Next Door*, two young women with seemingly vastly different lives end up forming an unexpected and heart-warming connection. In Selma Dabbagh's devastatingly touching and intense short stories *Take Me There* and *Last Assignment to Jenin*, romantic love (problematic though it may be) is shown to have a place even in the most unjustly besieged of locations. The poems of Imtiaz Dharker fizz with irony, cheekiness and a determination to challenge the status quo. Miss L's *Stand By Me* is a hilarious but saddening account of trying to follow her dreams of becoming an actor as a British woman of Middle-Eastern heritage. It shows how far the creative industries – who often like to think of themselves as more progressive than others – have to go in terms of widening the representation of non-white people, especially minority women.

Important themes are tackled in this anthology, sometimes explicitly, as in the case of Shaista Aziz's searing *Blood and Broken Bodies*, a damning account of honour killings in Pakistan. Aisha Mirza's viscerally absorbing memoir of following the EU Referendum far from home, *Staying Alive Through Brexit: Racism, Mental Health and Emotional Labour*, succinctly explores many of the difficult issues the title suggests. They are also presented in more subtle ways, shown through the apposite choice of metaphor, geographical backdrop and character in Hibaq Osman's collection of poems, one of which also provided the title for this anthology. They are there in each line of dialogue in Leila Aboulela's play *The Insider*, set in Algeria, which follows some of the Arab characters featured briefly in Albert Camus's *The Outsider* through the ages to the modern day.

In creating this anthology, it was vitally important to me that the reader was offered a range of narratives and writing styles – fiction, memoir, opinion, poetry, drama – that reflect the breadth and richness of these women writers' work. The narratives take place across the globe: the authors take us from Karachi to Algiers, Palestine to New York, Yemen to Somalia and, eventually, we end up rooted in Britain.

Through these different mediums we meet characters such as Hanan al-Shaykh's Tareq in *An Eye That Sees*, a Yemeni attendant at the V&A Museum in Kensington; the Iraqi children born in the aftermath of Britain's bombing of Fallujah in Shazea Quraishi's poetry; and the young women who are digitally searching for love in Triska Hamid's exploration of *Islamic Tinder*. Fadia Faqir's Doris, in the short story *Under the Cypress Tree,* is a delightful seaside character grappling with ageing, death, a constantly changing Britain and the alien Bedouin with special powers, who moved in next door. Throughout her poems, Azra Tabassum presents varied and intimate reflections of family members and the emotions their expectations elicit. We go to the Midlands with Aliyah Hasinah Holder's poems, which include a bruising account of the effect of a private prison opening in the local area. These writers all offer an energising and eye-opening exploration of people and place, whatever medium they employ.

It was also important to include a mix of authors in terms

of renown and experience. The anthology celebrates literary heavyweights such as Ahdaf Soueif, Kamila Shamsie, Leila Aboulela, Fadia Faqir and Hanan al-Shaykh. Between them, they have been short- or long-listed for four Orange Prizes, two Man Booker Prizes, and have won countless other awards and accolades for their work.

Alongside these renowned authors are emerging and new voices of British women of Muslim heritage. Writers such as Chimene Suleyman, Hibaq Osman, Aisha Mirza and Samira Shackle are published and respected writers who work internationally, yet they are at the early stages of their careers and bring exceptional energy and experimentation to the pages that follow. Aliyah Hasinah-Holder, Asma Elbadawi, Nafeesa Hamid and Amina Jama are tremendously talented writers published here for the first time. In spite of their young ages, their work is complex and compelling. Asma Elbadawi and Amina Jama, at only eighteen years of age, were winners of a nationwide search in 2015 by BBC 1xtra and The Roundhouse for the best new performance poets. They spent a year being mentored by The Roundhouse in London and their work has since featured on radio, TV and online. Though she is still at university, Nafeesa Hamid's honesty and observations are dynamic and thought-provoking.

The contributors in this collection are an inspirational force. The fact that these women all have a British identity and a Muslim heritage is important, as the canon we are handed down and much of what is taught at school do not always provide those from diverse backgrounds with an opportunity to find writing that resonates with their own experiences. Nor does it lead them to writers who share similarities of background with them, allowing them to know that it is possible for them to write, to be published, to perform, to be read.

I work with girls and young women at schools, as well as with charitable organisations all over the world, and I have been stunned by the difference it has made to the writing of those who wear the hijab, for example, to watch a YouTube video of a young woman wearing a hijab and reciting her poetry on stage. Seema Begum, who was fourteen years old at the time, wrote her poem *Uomini Cadranno* in one such workshop. She demonstrates how negative stereotypes can be defeated through the written word. It never fails to surprise me how much representation can empower and how much non- or misrepresentation can disempower. We should never underestimate this, and we must do whatever we can to challenge the current dominant narrative. Through the vast variations of style and content that exist in this anthology, I hope you find that the following pieces all do exactly that.

London

Destroy the whole world
But leave London for me,
For it is here I feel at ease,
It is here that I am free.

Triska Hamid

Fadia Faqir

Under the Cypress Tree

She stepped out into the morning mist, a dark cloud extending and gathering like a swarm of flies. A veil, fixed with a band, covered her head and the collar of her padded jacket. The hem of her sharwal visible under her loose-fitting robe, her shoes flat. She shook the dust off her saddle bag, gathered her fardels and looked up. When Doris saw her weather-beaten skin, kohled-eyes and tattooed chin she held her breath and stepped back away from the window. A puff of cold air blew on Doris's face. She blinked. All these layers of blackness, honestly. If she squatted next door she would bring the whole neighbourhood down to the level of whichever manhole she had crawled out of. Perhaps a bag lady with all of them colourful cloth bundles. How do you measure?

The war had started. They were at the Marigold when her father spilt the tea on his crotch. He ran to the gents, swearing. Full of sugar it was hot and sticky. Suddenly her mother's mood changed. Grey clouds rushed and gathered across the sky. Later her father, stocky and assured, sat on a deckchair smoking his pipe. He was a collier on the jetty and was given a few days break in Brighton. He came home tired, his eyes watering, lips tight, shirt black and shoe covers caked with dark mud. They overheard the couple on the next table talk about barbed wire on the shore and fortifications. It was pelting down when they ran back to the guesthouse carrying their beach bags and rugs.

What with German bombers flying low above their heads Doris rarely stepped out of her flat. The most she did was water the lavender plant on the landing. She had to be extra careful now. While fiddling with the decorations something blocked the light and cast its shadow on the floor. It went cold, a chill that penetrated the very marrow of your bones. She had swirls and stars tattooed on her chin and she wore a few turquoise stones stringed together. Little cloth bags full of God-knows-what and feathers were knotted to her belt. The smell of dung and incense rose up.

The crone's teeth were yellow. 'Good morning! The weather not bad today.'

Doris pushed her glasses up and rubbed her arms. 'Good morning.'

She put the broom down. 'I Bedouin. Name Timam, your neighbour.'

Primitives rolled their eyes and bared their teeth on telly, somewhere in North Africa.

'I go to market later, do you want anything?' Her gold-clad tooth caught the sun.

Doris ran out of milk and bread. She hesitated. 'No, thank you.'

Timam persevered. 'What a lovely day! Cold, but sun. Is this Christmas tree?'

What did she bleeding know about Christmas, fresh from the desert? 'Glad you like it.'

Timam sucked her teeth. 'Honour meeting you.'

Doris slammed the door then locked and bolted it. Out

of breath she sat on her favourite chair, right next to the gas fire and adjusted the crochet covers on the armrests. She checked her memorabilia: a black and white photo of her in a swimming suit and sunglasses next to a handsome man in uniform, another of a dog, a porcelain Russian ballerina, and Winston Churchill wearing a hat, a white suit, a poppy in his lapel, holding a walking stick. She also read the list of important phone numbers: 999 for emergencies, doctor's surgery, the Local Council, DineWise elderly food delivery.

She fiddled with the knob of her temperamental radio until classical music floated out, a breeze of notes. Listening to the *Waves of the Danube*, she stretched her hands against the fire. It was spring. She was waltzing in a ballroom with a wooden floor and chandeliers with a man she barely knew. 'A dance of too loose character for maidens to perform.' Her narrow-waist taffeta dress tightened against her ribcage, restricting her breathing. A click of a lens. A young woman with blonde hair, red lips and dark eyelashes, legs shimmering in nylon tights, a cigarette in one hand and a glass of crème de cacao and gin in the other, leaning on the balcony of the King Alfred pub, watching the soldiers rushing in in herds. She lowered her glasses and ran her eyes over John's waxed hair, large blue eyes, silly big ears and thin lips. With the back of her sleeve she wiped the glass frame and put the photo back on the side table. Spans. Spoons.

'Insert two slices of bread in the toaster and watch them brown!' Something that started with 's' she ran out of often, a powder she knew she really liked. You spoon it then add it to tea. There was no milk in the fridge so she buttered the toast, put it with the mug of tea on a tray and took it to the sitting room. She switched the television on, had a sip then shouted, 'Sugar!'

The bell rang. The dark crone from upstairs stuck her face to the door viewer. 'Move away! I cannot see you!'

Timam stepped back and sucked her teeth.

Doris slid the safety chain open and unlocked the door. 'What do you want?'

She flicked a green aromatic substance between her teeth. 'I bought you milk from the old market. Here you are!' She pushed it against her.

'Are you chewing your snot? Honestly!'

'No! How do you say? Cardamom!'

'I see. . .' Doris hesitated as she ran her fingers on the misty surface of the plastic bottle. She looked away then faced the beady kohled-eyes. 'Thank you! That should do!'

Timam gathered her robe and skittered away.

Caddy jumped up then nibbled her foot. A black stocky dog, with a broad head, round eyes, small ears, saggy skin, that kept licking his snotty nostrils with his pink tongue. He waddled after her. The fire was lit and the kitchen was warm. Doris's mother, still in her hat and coat, was drinking her Milo malt and cocoa and reading a magazine the lady she worked for in Chelsea had given her. Doris was eating a slice of cake and throwing the crumbs to Caddy. He chased them, collected them with his tongue then ate them snorting. 'Don't give him your food,' her ma said and turned the page. 'He's so fat his tiny legs can barely carry him.'

'But mother, he's hungry.'

'I just fed him the bones of yesterday's broth.' She inspected the magazine.

Caddy licked her bare feet and looked up, pleading. She threw down bits of cake.

'You'll not get your copper if you continue spoiling that dog.'

'The way he looks at me, ma.'

Her dark hair was pulled back and neatly tucked under a round red hat, the buttons of her coat undone and her feet rested on the stool. She was reading loudly a recipe for pudding with cherries and custard. The rations wouldn't stretch that far. Did they have any eggs?

Doris lost things quite often. She was looking for her glasses when she heard the knock on the door. 'Go away!'

'Please, Madam, open the door.'

The muffled voice of that dreaded woman!

'I know you in there. Open the door! I have milk. It might sour.'

She stood by the window. A few black birds, perched on a chimney cowl, necked and then flew away. Doris opened the door.

Timam's jacket was covered with snow flakes. 'Here you are!'

'I can't find my glasses,' Doris blurted.

Timam smoothed her long robe. 'Don't worry. I find for you.'

Doris, hesitated, stepped back and allowed her to cross the threshold.

The stink of sheep dung and the scent of something pleasant like eucalyptus filled the room.

Timam ran her hands on the sofa, coffee table, side table, television set and the carpet. 'May I go to bathroom?'

'You want to use it?' Doris panicked.

'See glasses.'

'Yes, yes.' She pressed her white muslin handkerchief over her nose.

'Here they are! I wiped them real good.'

Doris put her glasses on, ran her fingers through her hair, stood up then buttoned her cardigan. 'That would do. Thank you.' She opened the front door.

Timam sucked her teeth, gathered her robe and went out. The war had started. Doris convulsed on the bed. The muscles of her arms and legs went into spasms and her back arched. Her temples were raw, saliva ran down her chin and her eyes spun as if she had just finished a big wheel ride at the fun fair. An incubator. White walls, sheets, a bed, a cabinet and a light bulb. The stench of disinfectant, vomit and urine filled her nostrils. Her forehead was covered with a thin layer of a foul-smelling paste. It was high voltage this time. When it hit her gums, it rattled her teeth. Was she caught in the blast? The reek of burnt flesh, leaking gas, powdered brickwork, and explosives filled the air. The sound of sirens, men shouting at each other, the crunch of broken glass underfoot and the crying of babies. She could hear the whistle of workers outside, smell concrete and fresh paint, and taste dust on her furry tongue. There was a presence in the room, a woman in a white uniform.

'I can't control me right hand. It keeps jumping about,' Doris whispered.

'Say that again.'

'I can't feel me head.'

'Come again!'

'Me hand has gone into spasms.' Doris swallowed.

'Don't worry! It'll calm down,' the woman in white said.

'Was I caught in the blitz?'

'You could say that.' She giggled.

'Is he still on the front?'

'Is your lover boy back?'

A blast then blood, thick and warm, ran down her thighs. Her father pelted her. She steadied herself, shifted her weight and faced the wall. Cracks. The window panes, filthy and held together with sticky tape, kept the light out. Spoons. Dry-eyed and slimy, she hissed like a lizard.

Timam kept knocking on the door. 'It me your neighbour from upstairs.'

Doris opened the door and stood there, blocking the

entrance. 'What do you want?' Her skin was dark and leathery, her nostrils flared and her chin tattooed with swirls and stars. The colour of ink.

'I brought you something.'

'Why? Is it Christmas already?' She fumbled with her shirt buttons.

'No. Not yet. But because you old lady.' Timam stuck the gleaming bag in her hand.

'You better come in.' She stepped back.

Doris sat on the armed chair, opened the gift bag and pulled the scarf out. 'It's beautiful. All that embroidery!' She ran her hand over it.

'Belongs to great grandmother.'

'Different shapes and patterns.'

'Each mean something. Direct to a place. Like a life.'

Direct to a place. If only her English was better. 'Thank you. It's lovely.' Doris pointed at the other armed chair.

Timam sat on the edge and adjusted her headband.

'Do you want a cuppa?' She rubbed her arthritic knee then stood up.

'Yes, please.'

Doris came back with a cup of tea and some biscuits on a tray. She pulled a nest of tables and put the smallest in front of her.

Timam held the cup in both hands, had a sip then spat out. 'So bitter.' She added four spoons of sugar, stirred, drank and smiled, baring her yellow teeth.

The primitives ululated and hopped in the air. Doris settled in her chair, holding the gift bag. 'How're you finding living here then?'

'Good. It so cold.'

'That's British weather for you.' Kohl ran down the corners of her eyes like tears, her skin was rough and her shoes were dirty and worn out.

'Although it cold the sun shinning.'

'Oh! Yes! It is a typical autumn day.' Doris bit on her dentures.

'Perhaps we can go out. Say goodnight to everything.'

Goodnight. Honestly! 'I never visited my mother's grave.' Doris didn't know why she said that. She stood up, took the cup out of Timam's hand and put it on the saucer. 'Thank you for your gift. It's time for me to have my lunch.'

Timam wrapped her padded jacket around her and went out.

It was a sunny day and Doris was getting ready to go out. Don't worry about the bombs! Come to the Café de Paris! Doris was leaning on John's arm outside.

'Are you ready?'

'Yes.' Her heart thudded in her chest.

John held her hand and followed the usher to a table upstairs by the banister. The stars on his shoulder caught the light. Doris sat, smoothed down her dress, and wiped her forehead. How did the cigarette girls keep their hair so tightly curled? They must have paid a fortune to get it permed.

'What would you like to drink?' John's eyes glistened as if they were full of tears.

'Can I have cream de cacao please?'

'Why don't we start with champagne, darling? We don't get to listen to Ken Johnson's band every day.'

'They call him "snakehips".'

'Do they?'

'He danced so well in *Oh Daddy*!'

When John finished ordering the drinks and hors d'oeuvre he offered her a cigarette. She fidgeted in her chair. He watched her pull it out, fiddle with it then place it between her lips.

'Let's dance!' he said like an afterthought.

The clanking of cutlery, animated conversation and piano

music travelled to her ears. She wanted to show him Brighton. It was dark and the lights of the pier were reflected in the water, colourful and elongated. They stood bare-foot on the shore listening to the waves rustle along pebbles and sand then retreat back to the sea. His lips touched hers for the first time, a fleeting peck. He got closer, took off his cap, and kissed her so hard she felt his teeth grate against hers. The jolly sound of diners singing along to 'It's a Lovely Day Tomorrow' was carried by the breeze to where they stood embracing, there on the shore by the barbed wire. Yards.

Doris showered, powdered herself with red rose perfume talc, pushed her dentures in and bit, put her glasses on, got dressed then opened the sitting room curtains, allowing the sunshine in. She was about to settle in her settee when the door bell rang. It was her neighbour in her full Bedouin regalia.

'It me your neighbour Timam.' She tilted her head backward.

'Are you off to Her Majesty's garden party at Buckingham Palace? All dressed up like that!'

'No. I go to baker and butcher in the market. Do you buy anything?'

'Did you say the baker?' She pushed her glasses up.

'Yes. Frightened man.' Timam sat down on the sofa.

'My mother loved the old-fashioned English custard tarts with thick wobbly filling. She loved the nutmeg flavour and the crisp pastry.'

'I ask the baker. He will get for me if not in shop.' She squatted in front of Doris and held her hands. The scent of acacia rose up. 'You say you never go to your ma's grave. We arrange visit.'

'We arrange a visit to my mother's grave?' Doris freed her hands and pulled the collar of her shirt up.

'Yes. We go together?' Timam sucked her teeth.

'Let me think about it. Here is some money.' She took a five-pound note out of her purse.

'No money!'

'Take the money! I'll write down that I'd given you five pounds so I won't forget.'

'No money. Later.' She gathered her robe and went out.

Doris settled in her settee and began watching morning television. A doctor described the dangers of having sexual intercourse at an early age. 'Young girls are not ready for it both physically and mentally.' Her cheek was soft against her breasts, taut with milk. Chinese silk. Her eyes wandered. Just out of her, she was warm and clingy, clasping her fingers and toes around your arm like a hydra fresh out of a pond. Before her lips met her nipples, they put her up for adoption. Must not get too attached. An officer came round and found John's face, which was blasted off, stuck over his shoulder. In electric shocks.

The painting of the oil jetty on the river Thames, hung above the fireplace, was grim. The silhouette of the cast-iron pillars of the jetty was dark against the sky and on the right a small boat was heading out to the shore. Her father used to work there. His eyes were bloodshot and his face covered with black dust when he held her tight and shook her. 'You got your rocks off. Didn't you?' He then belted her. The buckle dug right into her side. Her skin bruised and flailed, she sat on the floor crying. 'She's not my daughter. I disown her. A harlot. That's what she is.' Her mother cried in the kitchen. Doris could hear her snivels. Caddy licked her feet.

Then she went away. Her ma sent her a letter. 'I know how hard it is. Please hang on there, Doris. Caddy is missing you. He barks right into the night and stays outside waiting for you. I hear laughter in the bedroom and when I go to check you're not there. What happened to us?' Almost a year later she visited her and gave her the plate as a gift. She used to sneak in on her way back from work for a few minutes. Once she came when Doris was really bad. Her head was shaven and her forehead smeared with a blue paste. She kissed her. 'Take care of yourself chuck!' She never saw her again.

Timam knocked on the door, screaming, 'The taxi here, mortal Doris.'

Mortal, honestly? Doris opened the door. Timam stood there, panting. Doris straightened her arthritic knee, held her walking stick and trudged out of the building for the first time in years. She stood on the pavement and breathed in the fresh air laden with the smell of grass and trees. She hadn't seen all that brightness for a long time. Some you forget and others you remember. The warmth of the sun on her shoulders loosened them.

'Taxi driver foreign friend. He very good and reasonable.' Timam held the door open.

Doris sat in the back, put her walking stick against the front seat, put the plate, the custard tart and the letter in her lap and tidied up her hair. Timam gathered her layered attire and squeezed herself next to her.

When they settled in the taxi, the driver, a black man, looked in the front mirror. 'Are you alright, girls?'

Girls! Girls! Honestly. Doris wound down the window and inhaled.

Shifting her weight onto the stick, Doris shuffled through the cemetery's gate. Sycamore trees with ivy-wrapped trunks rose high, blocking the light of the sun. Blackberry bushes grew everywhere and the ground was blanketed with nettles.

'We look, look for your mother's grave until we find. What her name?' Timam fingered the cloth bags, bottles and dry twigs tied to her belt.

'Jane Robson was her married name. Her maiden name was Jane Asher.'

Timam scanned the sky.

'Oh! Look the grave of Alexander Hurley!' You could still read the writing although the headstone was cracked and chipped.

'Who?'

'The comedian who sang the 'Lambeth Walk'. My mother used to listen to him on the wireless. Perhaps we will find her here.'

They followed the footpath among oak, beach and hazel trees, careful not to step on the flowering primroses.

'Look crows want for food!' Timam pointed at four black birds.

'We'll never find her in this bush. Look at it. Grass, weeds, trees everywhere. Like looking for a needle in. . . in. . .'

'Don't worry, we find it. We stay all day.'

They sat down on the ground exhausted. Doris's hip and knee throbbed with a dull pain. It was getting dark and the wind picked up, bringing a chill with it.

'I can hear starlings. They mimic noise, squeak, click.' Timam looked up.

'How do you know that?' Doris buttoned up her coat.

'Just know.' She rubbed the leaf of a weed then sniffed her fingers.

Perhaps they should go back. She may be buried in another cemetery. How would she know? She cast the net of her mind far and wide and it came back empty. Blank except two fingers clasping a photograph of a cake.

Timam held Doris's hand. It felt rough and warm against her skin. 'We look again. Heart says we will find.'

Doris sighed and wiped the sweat off her forehead. That pain. This life. Measure if you dare.

They stood up and went through the overgrowth to the farthest corner of the walled cemetery, where the blackberry bushes were high and entangled. Timam parted the weeds and nettles with her bare hands and strode on. Doris stopped and pointed her walking stick at a grave you could hardly see. There it was! A humble headstone with 'Jane Asher 1902–1958. May she rest in peace' carved on it.

Timam kneeled down, spread her hands behind her ears, clicked her teeth, chanted a few foreign verses, blew on the grave then skittered away into the bush.

Was the crumbling headstone made of sand or lime? Could she restore the curve to the edges? Perhaps she could come one day and clear the area; get rid of the grass, bushes and weeds. Plant a geranium or two. Doris knelt down, put the custard tart on the plate, the letter on top and placed them carefully on the ground. 'You don't know how important the plate was to me. The two orange flowers drawn on each side, the grey foliage, and circa 1932 Tudor Ware were imprinted behind my eyeballs. Some things you cannot remember and others you cannot forget. Sixteen. Not my age. Electric shocks. I held on to the image of orange flowers until they turned into an open meadow, green, dew-covered, and dotted with forget-me-nots.'

Doris tried to conjure up her features, remember the colour of her eyes, the tilt of her head. All she could see was an image with the face cut out. Just her slim fingers holding the magazine and the red beret on her head. The nurses advised her to take a deep breath. She inhaled. Nothing. What about John's? The name of the plant with delicate yellow flowers? Which word would describe that tall trunk with branches and leaves?

'Where am I?' Doris snivelled.

'It time depart.' Timam leapt out of the bushes and stuck the herbs she had gathered in different bags.

He must be resting under the cypress tree. Timam was cleaning Doris's kitchen one morning when he arrived. She was expecting him. He whirled through the window past her. A thud. She rushed to the sitting room and found Doris on the floor, gasping for air. She lay there like a slain bird with her nightgown wrapped around her thigh. Grey-faced, clammy, she convulsed on the floor. Timam pulled the Fear Beaker out of her bundle, filled it with water, added some drops of orange blossom then blew on it. She helped Doris drink.

Doris saw the foreign words etched on the brass, the letters hooked to its edge, yet she drank then closed her eyes. A piercing pain in her chest, there where the ribs meet. Her windpipes tightened. Alone, in a dingy flat, besieged by foreigners. 'Oh!'

Timam brewed a drink and gave it to Doris. The aroma of herbs was strong and sickly. She held the warm cup and had a sip. It was as bitter as barberry, but Doris had no option. She had to drink it.

Timam squatted on the floor and put Doris's head on her thigh. 'Relax! Breathe deep!'

Doris rasped, 'My heart is beating. Chest tight. Cannot.'

'Let go now. You say goodnight to your mum, to the streets.' She stroked her hair, humming and muttering, until she went limp. Timam carried her to the sofa, took off her glasses, covered her with a blanket and adjusted her head on the pillow. A few minutes before she died she whispered something Timam could not understand. 'Tell John I'll meet him at the King Alfred. I'll take Caddy with me. My ma was still missing. Keep the photos, plate and letter!'

'Yes. Do your wishes.' Timam sucked her teeth.

Her beady eyes were so close to Doris' face she could see the honey-flecked irises. Two ink-coloured lines crossed her cracked lower lip. Never mind. Was her mother's name Jane Asher? What about her? Was she Doris Robson? She nodded.

The grass glistened with dew. Bluebells all the way from lavender to purple. Not to be confused with the hybrid breed. In the number of petals you plucked and counted. Droopy.

Timam held her. 'Don't tired yourself! Everything fine. Just breathe easy! We meet again!'

'Meet again?' Doris opened her eyes. A summer sky covered with hazy clouds.

'Yes. Other end.' She clicked her tongue.

Doris relaxed on the pillow and rubbed her fingers together for the very last time.

'Must help.' Timam pushed the band off her sweaty forehead and sat on the floor rocking and keening.

Doris gasped her last breath. It was an easy delivery this time.

When the sun sat and darkness spread Timam stood up, pressed her finger on Doris's jugular, lowered her lids, covered her face and smoothed out the blanket. How many sunrises had she seen? How many harvests? Now she would follow the river to the sea, dance to the wind, rushing through the leaves. Now she was free, her heart whole.

Timam put Doris's photograph, her mother's letter and the plate in her saddle bag. She had enough bugloss, alkanet, lion's foot, pomegranate peel, aloe, colocynth to last her years. She checked the oils in the bottles, eucalyptus, tea tree, bergamot, valerian, sassafras and the peacock and black hen feathers. She put the Fear Beaker back in the bundle, tied it, balanced it on her head, and left.

Note: Timam is an Arabic name. It and its derivatives mean completion of a cycle, ending and finishing a task.

Amina Jama

Home, to a Man

Home, to a man

A home without breasts is just a house

Nooks and crannies need to be cleared,
mother taught me
never to be envious of others' houses
they only wish to break down yours,
men wish to break it down

I'm the lucky one,
I know that much
but I can feel the paint peeling
from the bathroom walls.
I don't know what I'll do
when it finally falls

Nooks and crannies need to be cleared,
Mama told me to never give away
my spare keys

that it is sacred between God and I,
but she makes a pair for any
wealthy man arranging a visit

Mama refuses to buy sanitary towels
in the household shopping
She asks *what will you do*
if your brothers see them,
if they see that your house is dirty?
She says *Hishod naya,*
Have shame, girl.

Nooks and crannies need to be cleared,
I once turned off all the lights
I swear I felt my soul leave the house,
I said *Good for you girl!*
You deserve to be happy

Nooks and crannies must be cleared.
When a man comes to view your house
it must be clean.
Don't just sweep
the dirt under the carpet.
Trim
that rug.
Make sure all your corridors
are clear of impurities

Make sure your living room is presentable,
it is the bosom of your home.
Stay in the kitchen or the bedroom,
mama tells me,
so he can watch you in your
natural habitat

Mama taught me I must
speak my mind, though
every man is allowed to test
out my home before he buys it.
So if he wants to inspect,
let him beg to witness all your rooms
and if he breaks down your walls,
give in, maybe

Mama taught me to be wary
of handing him all my glory at once.
He must also do some polishing of edges.

Nooks and crannies must be cleared.
Perhaps,
by a man.

Examples of confusion

An uncut woman
is not a clean woman,
the nurse translated, meant to say
the doctor needs to open you up
the stitches were done too tight, everything
will be ok.
Meant to say
meant to
but said *mada hishod haysanin*:
don't you have no shame?

The scar healed wrong,
layers of skin grew but never closed it up.

You should feel ashamed of
what they don't know.

He's always on the ward for dying patients, you said
how does he make it past the angel of death each night?
It feels awkward
to use my full name,
it's too immigrant to say out loud.
They argued on what to call me,
he wanted a name that I couldn't run away from,
she wanted a three-dimensional one.
Said I was her Luul,
carved and sculpted in the womb, too precious
to let go.

She gave in.

The drive to Heathrow was grey
somehow Londoners call this summer,
they don't know that warmth is in colour.

Why does leaving feel like the coast, bare?

Mum's laugh is recorded
over Zainab's wedding tape,
and I realise it's not as I remember.

Fire

They wonder how you made something of yourself.
You told them that you stopped dwelling
on what could have been
because it was exactly that – could have –

They see you standing in the park
muttering to pink pigeons and crisp packets,
as if communicating with them was easier
than your family.

They call your speech urban, but
it's scratching at things that shouldn't be
scratched, and when it does, it sounds like
extinguishers crying.

The council flat you were a girl in has had its doors fixed,
now
the tenants can sleep with both eyes closed, not
hold your fear of him climbing up you
while you're trying to dream.

They call your dreams urban, but
The doctor who told you that your nineteen-year-old boy
died from a stroke, makes eye contact on the 25 bus.
You cling to your bag, ignore

that you're back in that white ward, that white room,
that white-white moment – and
nod in his direction. Get off
before the big Asda, before even the station.

They call our love urban, but
You don't cry at your son's funeral,
or on his birthday. No, you mourn
the anniversary of his first football match.

They call our grief urban, but
the man who said he loves you, wraps
his arms around the waist of someone
less damaged. Don't care

until you do, until you are
standing outside his house
holding a full glass of water.

Chimene Suleyman

Cutting Someone's Heart Out with a Spoon

Cutting someone's heart out with a spoon would be an unwise thing to do. For a number of reasons. Firstly, it is not specified whether the body is already open; the spoon's only job to scoop heart out. Or if it is expected to first manoeuvre through skin as well. This would be far harder and an ongoing job, limiting the feelings of satisfaction that you may have been expecting.

Spoons are fine, however, if you are balancing cutlery on your nose, eating ice-cream, or performing a regular autopsy.

– Couldn't find nothing else?

– No.

– In your kitchen, couldn't find nothing?

– No. I looked.

In the plastic bag are six spoons, the plastic case of a ballpoint pen, and half a spliff, charred and folding at the end.

– In your kitchen? For real? Nothing?

Kyle's fingers are dirty. The graze beside his mouth, from where his aunt's cat scratched him earlier, is drying in the sun. Jack shrugs. He says his mother caught him going through her bedroom, like a pervert, for any cutlery she'd left in dinner plates that she had eaten in bed. So he had grabbed what he could on the way out.

– Washing-up weren't done, was it.

– What are we going to do with these?

When Kyle is cross his nose flares. The right nostril enlarges a little and pulsates. Jack refuses to give in.

– You said we were gonna do it like diggin.

– You're a fuckin idiot.

The space between their flats is tarmac, a low wall and a swing. Five floors of brown brick turn around itself, a row of red doors along each outside corridor. Black drainpipes run along the double-glazing. Few have bothered with pot-plants. It is the same on every side. A child's pink bicycle collapsed, the colour fading from weather.

Above courtyard, taller buildings peer. The brightness of Canary Wharf, unmissable, only a mile into their eye-line. The pyramid stretches – One Canada Square is higher than the Barclays and HSBC beside. In the middle of the courtyard, by the locked bicycle with the missing front wheel, you can't see a building that isn't these. The communal green and black bins rest against one wall of their estate. The wall dips ever-so-slightly away from the yard, a small space with no windows along the height of it. The street on the other side disappears into the black railing. If you turn to look in that direction you may see Jack's legs stretched, the rest of his body out of sight against the building he is leaning into.

– If you don't want to use them, fuckin don't.

– Bit late now.

– Shu' up.

Kyle unfolds paper.

– It's a diagram. All mapped out here.

The outline is of a person. Round limbs, bloated where

shape should be. The organs are to the side of where would be correct and drawn in green biro.

– Got that science girl to do it, two years above, big tits.

– So where is it then?

– Near stomach, I guess.

An incomplete oval is circled, GALBLADER written to the side.

– My uncle ate his.

– Your uncle is full of shit.

– That's what my nan says.

Kyle squats low to the ground in jogging bottoms, white vest top and yellowing near the collar, tighter by the shoulders that are growing without his notice.

– It's sort of, sort of, here.

Jack sticks his finger into his side, through a thin pale jacket, tracksuit a little too short, a fat worm-scar running down the side of a shaved scalp that doesn't suit him.

– What if no one buys it?

Jack lies on the floor, body at an angle to fit the corner they are in. Kyle inspects green biro once more, runs his fingers across the page.

– Lift your top up.

Kyle drags the spoon across Jack's skin. The friction leaves a red mark, but little else happens. Skin moves, flattened on one side. It is possible no one will buy Jack's gallbladder. Kyle has considered this. He knows that if they get through the skin, using the diagram that was drawn for them, they may still not receive its worth. Kyle thinks about reminding Jack of the risks, weighing it all up, but he knows Jack will disagree. Jack will express certainty of his plan, remind Kyle it is fool-proof, a question at the end of his sentences, it's fool-proof, Kyle, it's fool-proof, it's fool-proof? Kyle?

They already have the bubble-padded envelope, A5, addressed; Mick Hucknall. Glenmore Estate. Donegal.

– What if he don't want it?

– Why wouldn't he?

– Your gallbladder?

– Ah'll tell him mum's got all his shit CDs, he'll have to buy it off me after that. Kyle sticks the spoon into Jack's stomach, jabbing it quick.

– Sit still you dick. Does it hurt?

– No.

– Does it hurt?

– No.

Kyle turns the spoon a different direction, drags it back, left, back, red, red, white, red, a red line across the area. His knees on the ground for better grip, the hand with the spoon dragging a pattern across his friend. Nothing changes, skin is raised but does not open. Skin is sore but stays in one piece. They repeat, back forward, left, Kyle's movements faster until his arm aches.

– This isn't fuckin worth it.

Kyle throws the spoon. Jack turns onto his side so he can reach where it has landed, dulled metal with white rice stains.

– She's wanted this fucking washing machine.

– Your mum's as big a prick as you.

– We'll get this fuckin thing out, sell it to Hucknall, then you don't need to do nothing. I'll take the money to shop myself.

Legs out in front, Jack moves his bottom until he is lying flat again, at an angle, he throws back the spoon. Kyle tips his head, a guiltiness in his lips, pressed together. He has poked holes at his friends plan without offering any suggestions of his own.

– Think he'll buy it, then?

– Guess so.

– Where'd she meet him?

– Hucknall? Dunno. Don't think she has. She don't leave the house enough. Plays his songs a lot.

– Why?

– Cos she likes em. You know, they talk or something. He's havin conversations with her in the words, or some shit like that. I'd give it all up for you, then she sings, Yeah, I would, I'd give it all up for you, yeah, I would.

– Dumb bindt.

– Fuck off.

– OK. What you gonna get her once we get the money?

– Zanussi, I reckon. Bosch seems alright.

Scoring a spoon energetically against skin won't break it. It will raise skin, slightly, blistered around the lines from the metal. The bins, black heavy lids, near where they are sitting do not smell today. The sun is bright. It is one of those summer days where city boys will fill Smollensky's and the All Bar One; they will flirt with girls from their office, or the offices near by, cold beers and white wines. Here the estate is empty. There is little point in flirting. The Bangladeshi mothers bring their children home from school together, a large crowd migrate the same journey. A few children play in the courtyard, picking toys abandoned the night before. A television plays from one window, a mother shouts for it to be turned down, the ice-cream van plays his song outside the estate.

– Try a little harder, Jack says. Kyle lifts, stabs Jack up and down with it,

– Like that, yeah, he is wincing.

– Not working,

– If you don't get it out, Jack says.

Kyle scratches with it, Jack moves his legs involuntarily in response.

– Stop moving,

– I'm not,

– Stop, with his other hand Kyle holds his legs down.

– I'm not,

– Stop,
– I'm not, Jack moves.
– Shall we try a different way? I'll run at you with it.
– OK.

Kyle stands, throws himself forward two steps, pushes the spoon hard as he lands. Jack pulls his knees up and rocks, – For fucks sake. Kyle looks at the diagram again with sore fingertips on dirty hands, he studies it. Jack rests on his elbows, watered eyes, his jogging bottoms marked from the ground, but only on one side.

Kyle runs the spoon against the ground as though sharpening it. He checks the green biro drawing for certainty. – Just do it. – Yeah. Kyle puts spoon to the red raised skin. He drags it across the spot, strikes with the spoon. He moves quickly, Jack's body stretching out, neck hunched, he moves, – Stay still, he moves, – stay still. Kyle's legs go either side of Jack's, holds his body down between his. – What if we don't get it out? Jack says. He is held there, his legs touching beneath his friend's, one hand grabbing at his side. He wants to move the spoon without getting in the way, pulls his body up the tarmac. Kyle climbs his body, Jack's hips between his knees, one hand open on Jack's skin. – Try harder, the spoon against him he pulls his top up higher, gives more flesh to help, – Just get it the fuck out.

Kyle's fingers are tight on the spoon as he moves quickly, drags it fast. He is concentrating, pushing it into Jack's skin on the same spot, small sideways movements that get quicker. Jack's hand is held away by his friend, escaped tarmac resting in the back of his arm. His shoulders pushed into ground, he raises his body. His feet and shoulders, the back of his head on tarmac as he lifts the rest of himself, pushes Kyle up with him, toes of shoes on floor. The handle bends, Kyle's stomach against the one beneath. He digs with the spoon, drags it sideways and back, rubs, his face close to chest and they are both breathing.

His knees scrape, Jack's body drops back against it. Jack rolls to his side and again, Kyle moving with him, the spoon never leaves skin. Jack's hand in his, fingers closing into the other. – I'm trying, Kyle says slowly, gently, the stem of the spoon digging into his chest for strength. He rests his head against Jack's stomach, one knee now under his. They are breathing, face on skin, when he gives up.

They stay like this. Jack lying across ground, Kyle's ear near spoon-marked skin, his head in Jack's hand, his hair between Jack's fingers.

A tree grows out of gravel and blinks the sun through it, – We've got the envelope, nothing to put in it. A few clouds park over their heads. – Got nothing to sell. Kyle doesn't move his head, stretches his arm and puts the green-biro diagram into the envelope.

– Give him this.

– That stupid drawing?

– It's a picture of my gallbladder, alright? I said she should draw it of me, so send him that. I don't need it, have mine.

The plastic bag doesn't blow away, held by its insides including the case of a ballpoint pen to suck the gallbladder out and an A5 bubble-padded envelope addressed, 'Mick Hucknall, Glenmore Estate, Donegal'. Neither boy moves. Kyle's hair is wet from his sweat and lifted lightly in Jack's hand, Jack's stomach moves Kyle's head up, then back down. – Don't tell anyone about this. – I guess not. – They'd laugh if they heard we'd used a spoon.

A woman turns her head around the corner, looks at the buildings towering above them. Her face calm, she takes a photo of the pyramid, the buildings surrounding it, until they are one. The ice-cream van plays his song outside. There is no sky here, only the windows of Docklands buildings that reflect it.

Chimene Suleyman

Us

The plastic handles dug into Madeeha's fingers. A small rip appeared near the bottom of the carrier-bag where a juice carton poked through. From the pavement the canal below looked grass-green, the fungi a still blanket across it. Two new-builds with metre-long balconies tucked between redbrick warehouses that functioned as offices. Back windows watched out onto water. Letterbox-red Royal Mail vans parked in a line, the wide clock-face of St Anne's behind them.

From beneath a black coat zipped high to his chin, his gut swelled. Bald, grey stubble appeared by his ears, a day old. To one side of him a younger man with a long face and blue eyes the colour of cold that set against the grey of his suit. On the other, a man with a tight navy tie let out a mean laugh. They would teach her a lesson. That's what they said when they stepped from the bus outside Lidl and she had walked in front of them. They would teach her a lesson, this hummus-eating, camel-shagging slut.

Such behaviour seemed tolerated; a form of 'cruel to be kind', so Madeeha and people like her could assimilate into a British way of life faster. It would be good for her. Why else bother arriving in a country if it weren't to embrace all of it? Every part of it. Did that include the suspicion too, she wondered. No matter. She had heard it all before: your people are terrorists, you fuck Bin Laden, go home, paki, go home. For only that week a man on the 135 had looked at her and in a sing-song voice chanted, 'Kill them all. Kill them all. I don't give a fuck, kill them all.'

'Are we all responsible?' she had asked her husband. 'All billion of us? Is it my fault there's terror in this world? Did Muslims introduce terror to these people, like they had never acted in it before? Is it my fault, or is it yours?' For once something was not her husband's fault. And had he chosen to answer her he would have pointed it out with pleasure. But he hadn't responded. What could he say? This man who had worked in a butcher's for 18 years, who had missed family weddings and funerals, unable to pay for a flight, who now remembered more of Poplar than where he had once been born.

'They want us to apologise,' he said eventually, words mumbled between mouthfuls of bread.

'For what? Did I orchestrate the killings? Or think they are good? Innocent until proven guilty. Unless you are Muslim and they forget which order the saying goes.'

With bags of shopping in her hands, Madeeha was guilty until proven innocent: she hated British people and cheered the deaths of western journalists and soldiers. She had information on future acts of terror and could conceal a weapon beneath her garments. Truth was irrelevant, even proof wasn't required. This backwards, barbaric society she belonged to, for didn't they treat their women appallingly? And yet the man in the grey suit gripped the back of her arm.

'Don't.' she said.

'Fuck off.'

'Please don't.'

The man with the tie grabbed his belt buckle and she pushed the thought away. 'Please.'

'Why you even here? Terrorist bitch,' he shook her arm. The carrier bag split wider, a lemon fell from it and rolled into the road, 'fuck off back home and stop killing us.'

Us. She had heard this word so much. 'Us' did not come alone. 'Us' was paired with 'They'. They are uncivilised. They are brutal. They are savage. 'They' had accomplices: 'Them' and 'Those'. What did I tell you about those people? You know you can't trust them. This wasn't racism. No, it was self-preservation. No one was going to die because political correctness had spiralled into madness and if that meant hurting someone's feelings in order to be vigilant at an airport, or train station, supermarket, or road, then so be it.

'Please.'

The open palm pushed into her back. She caught her breath, the bags dropped spinning into traffic. On her knees she felt the grit rub against her skin. It stung. 'Fuck jihad. Islam is a cancer.'

Brown Oxford shoes stepped past, heels clicked against pavement, hands in pockets that searched for warmth.

Madeeha collected what she could: fruit, butter, meat that hadn't travelled far. She walked slowly. Yes, she was fine she insisted to passersby. She closed her front door and locked it. Spent a moment longer than she was used to with her back against it. Shireen was home. Music on, her daughter's voice became louder as she sang along. 'Mum? Is that you?' Us and Them. She thought on these words. Her daughter was both, but that wouldn't matter to them. That word again. Us and Them. Peace and Terror. Right and Wrong. Questions philosophers had centuries over been unable to answer and yet now everyone seemed to be so sure they knew. 'I am sorry.' She said these words into the house. Allowed them to find corners of cabinets to rest on; the photo frames; let them slow a moment over the cushions and the toaster and the rug. I am sorry. I am sorry for keeping you here. I am sorry you are not safe. 'Mu-uuum?' This is what it was to be afraid. 'I'm coming, my child.'

Aliyah Hasinah Holder

Sentence

Sentence

Chapter 1 – Mother

We lost you,
to roundabouts of social expectations
broken window experiments
and racist qualifications.
Lost you to fixed cycles. Rinsing at 90.

Thought you had to earn your stripes,
fit the mould of mass production,
bar-coded & branded.
Our sons checked in and out of our communities
like British weather.
An assimilation assembly line.

We lost you,
while we worked day and night
like stand upright,

don't argue. Don't fight.
Like eat the materialism you're fed, but avoid possession cuz
it'll offend
like black policemen get pulled over too
and we lost pieces of them to truncheons and boots.

Chapter 2 – Childhood friend

We're here again,
Hesitating by solid gates saying 'it don't matter it was gonna
happen anyway'

Men cling to confines mentally
women manhandled into the cells of their chromosomal
prophecy –
because diagnosis never leads to rehabilitation properly.
The 44% penned up before prescriptive security

We watched
like profit wouldn't make bricks of our backs again,
like please allow the Americanisation,
like do you really think the arrow has changed direction?

Chapter 3 – Pause

It's as if we live life in blindfolds gliding on paths towards man-
made destruction.
Gave us the dream pre-packaged in violence
allowed us to commodify our self-hate in words and creams
let it manifest surrounded by broken windows, empty plates &
superficial dreams.
Cracked systems, gauzed in supremacy, served us 38% more

JSA slips
and told us the issue was immigrants.

Chapter 4 – Girlfriend

And we lost you
to false masculinity fried into our plantain
we watched our black boys fly
only to have their feathers falter in a chemtrailed sky.

We lost love.
Somewhere between the failed GCSEs that were never
constructed with you in mind
and the arduous penalties for these petty crimes...

We lost you in legal fees and media perversion.

The lawyer assured us that justice would prevail
said bar the racial disparity
bar the profitable complexities
bar the background, the history, the psychology.

But we lost
gradually.

Chapter 5 – Inside

It was pennies for the pudding served on this tray.
But it was loaded cheques from Tony's Exchequer that made
G4S pay.
Now we see factories of punishment commodifying these
black lives.

Kept quiet. This hidden strife.

You don't change people through power.
You cannot beat obedience into our tired flesh.
Faux masculinity beating your chest, is the system flawed?
Is it Rehabilitative or Morally inept?

Chapter 6 – Sister

... there are 25 more stories balancing duty with expectation
in his corridor.
They grew to men too early
grasping juice cartons and part-time jobs.
Said our mum deserved better,
he'd shower her with precious rocks.

We rolled dice in summer's height once before,
we tried to fry eggs on Winson Green's tarmac floors,
scrambling it with plastic forks.
We lost brothers who traded innocence for scores.

Extended Edition. First commissioned by Channel 4 Random Acts.

New Blood

It's almost lunchtime, year 8 and I'm the new kid. All fresh off the hanger Blazer and pristinely oversised jumper. This one classroom holds the whole year and needs more maintenance than a crack whore. The roof is crying flakes of paint again. It smells of bubblegum lipgloss, PE kits, Impulse Musk and warm packed lunches.

Girls in sandpaper headscarfs sing out of tune.

Taylor Swift, our new Ustadha. She's teaching overactive hormones about love, the classist kind, in Restoration dresses with white boys who can only be described as wet. Every word out of tune makes our hearts feel a little more homeless.

Zaynah's chipping varnish off her nails again to avoid detention, its remnants under her nails taste of Palestine. Taste of dates, blood, rubble and hope. We dance in the corner, long skirts and scarves covering the bodies we've yet to discover. Hurriedly taped traffic cones stand guard by our sides, patronising in their warning to avoid the ceiling's depression. Buckets lap up the roof's disapproval. The music fluctuates.

We tap the volume on our phones to make sure Ustadha Saeda can't hear. She sent Latifah to scrub sin from her fingertips and temptation from her lashes. The books in her office threaten multiple lashes. She never hits us though. Muslims don't hit one another. We all wear transparent mascara now, think we've found routes to avoid uniform inspections. Our silent and invisible rebellion, our little slice of St Trinian's … And the twins are eating fried onion sandwiches at the back of the room again. Telling us it's haram to comment on food.

Dancing. Haram – only allowed on eid, weddings and special occasions.

Music. Haram – especially Taylor Swift.

Hair peeking through headscarf because of dancing and listening to music – definitely haram.

Then the popular girl, with her Taylor Swift CD and every teen *Vogue* copy, comments on how our dreams are the cuttings of glossed sheets. Says that the chips of our identity are new clothes and make up. She whips out notes in the canteen, she's an only child, apparently. Fiddles with silver strung wrist candy and waits for a full plate.

We were all Tyseley locomotive and floor-length black skirt. We were Paul's Boutique bags. We were weak chains of narration. We were condoms full of her dowry thrown by park trees before iftar. We were minds manufacturing A★s.

I was a third of the Caribbean plate in the year. Simran said I could call her a 'Paki' if I let her call me 'her Nigger'.

I did not.

We became brandy bottles staining warped window sills. We internalised the vitrole of vengeance, the direct path to Winson Green's private grimace, the broken feet of economics, the multi-lingual pots of bleach and caste. Wanting to trade slurs for street cred. We internalised it all. Prayed that all we'd fundraised, all the zakat we'd given, wasn't for posh desks and charity execs in the City – whose unsustainably shit models echoed the seats we sat in from 8am-4pm.

Too close to home. But our footsteps will testify. Walking home, I pass pussies pissing puddles on dead wasps. My security in the bullet holes of Aston's walls. Lost lottery tickets and crushed KA cartons made sure I remembered the route.

Mama made sure we were shipped out of the hood for school whilst Dad paid £6,000 a year to guarantee it. But we don't talk about how we can't afford it.

Latifah got caught smoking in the schoolyard again. Says she hopes Allah, but mainly the headmaster, will forgive her. In science I got a B+ for being a cheese sandwich. The journey down the trachea was the most eventful.

At least our history lessons make sense. Iraq War. Oil. Saddam. Hide. Al-Qaeda. Oil. Never sympathise in the exam. It's almost hometime, year 8 and I'm still the new kid.

This jumper keeps getting itchier.

Commissioned by Ten Letters theatre production.

Kamila Shamsie

The Girl Next Door

Noor was always the first to arrive.

The private guards at the gate waved her in without asking to see her security pass, and inside the main compound the young guard at the car-barrier - a long pole, lifted and lowered by means of a rope - pretended he was about to release the barrier to send it flying up between her legs as she stepped over it. She didn't mind, but the henna-bearded 'controller of drivers' looked up from the clipboard on which he was making complex charts of his drivers' schedules for the day and barked out a reprimand to the young guard. Noor liked the controller for never commenting on the obvious insincerity of her objection to the oft-repeated show of cheekiness. He was both the oldest and the most pious among the guards and drivers; his attitude acted as deterrent to any remarks from the others accusing her of immodesty.

The guard at the front door propped his rifle against the wall as he saw her approach, and extracted his keychain from his pocket, his fingers rather than his eyes allowing him to isolate the correct key – with large, wide-gapped teeth – in the pre-dawn gloom. That particular morning she was feeling bolder than usual, so she picked up his Kalashnikov by the barrel and swung it like a pendulum for a moment or two, until the weight of it made her drop it with an 'Uff!'

'A cotton bud has more strength' the guard laughed, holding the door open for her.

She knew she would go home and tell her sisters that the Pathan guard with the green eyes had called her 'cotton bud.' How they'd shriek!

Noor switched on lights as she made her way from the reception room through the open plan newsroom where dozens of sleeping computers hummed, and into the make-up studio. Her domain. Every other part of this two-year-old office was glass and chrome and shininess, but in this windowless cubbyhole there was another atmosphere - not of newness and technology, but of yearning. They all came through here, all Kyoon TV's guests and regulars - politicians, newscasters, comedians, cricketers, chefs, journalists, lawyers, maulanas, actresses, models, singers, artists, CEOs, VJs, everyone who was anyone, wannabes and coulda-beens, retired this and re-instated that. And in the end, whatever their different talents and opinions, they all wanted the same thing: to hide their blemishes from the world. That was where the yearning came from - it wasn't that they yearned to be liked or admired; they knew from the start that a portion of the viewers would automatically take against them based on whether they appeared 'too fundo' or 'too western', 'pro-army' or 'pro-sleazy-politicians', 'naive' or 'conspiracy-theorist', 'typical Muhajir' or 'typical Punjabi'. . . no, likability was not an option. But looking better on television than in real life, beaming out an image of themselves to the world which was preferable to the image which stared back at them from the mirror at the start and end of every day – that path remained.

And who did they rely on to put them on that path? Her – Noor, the girl with nothing more than a matric pass, though both her sisters were nurses at the grandest of Karachi's hospitals, the one where all the out-of-power politicians convicted of corruption went into private wards with air-conditioners when their doctors insisted they were too unwell to be kept in prison and had to be moved to a medical facility. Such celebrations went on inside those rooms, at all hours! - giant vats of biryani arriving daily to feed the party-faithful who stretched visiting hours in this direction and that. And one of her sisters had once been offered an entire month's payment if she would just lend her nurse's uniform and pass for one night to a woman who was obviously *that sort*. Though her sister was quick to add, she wasn't a cheap version of *that sort* but a very high-class one, and she'd chosen Noor's sister because she said the photograph on the i.d looked similar to her without make-up. Of course, her sister said, she hadn't taken the money – but she never explained how she was able to buy the new flatscreen TV for the family the following month.

Noor filled the electric kettle with mineral water – at home boiled water would do, but here only one brand of mineral water was acceptable – and went about the rest of her morning routine: switching on the lights which framed the mirrors above the two make-up tables, unlocking the drawer which contained her large cosmetics-case and hairbrushes, pulling out the strands of hair caught in the bristles and rolling them into a ball which she dropped into the trash can (really just an empty tin of cooking oil), switching on the wall-mounted television to MTV Pakistan, and finally settling down on one of the two cracked-vinyl swivel chairs with her cup of tea (with tea bag left inside to steep, so that by the final sips it would have reached optimum strength).

This was the best half hour of the day. Watching music videos, sipping hot tea, and anticipating which celebrities might come through the door that day. Most of all, it was the quiet she enjoyed. No eyes on her, no one looking and judging, no need to appear this way or that way. But by the time 5.30am came round, and she heard the sound of footsteps walking towards the make-up room, she was almost always ready to return to her true self, which was a creature of bustle over silence.

Some days were better than others. One day it could be all handsome actors and cricketers and a fashion designer commenting on the diamond-cut of her sleeves - and the next day nothing but newsreaders who had just left their villages two months ago and were now complaining about their blow-dries, followed by sudden pile-ups of six people who all needed to be made up in the next five minutes.

Today was middling all through the morning. But near 3pm when she thought the only thing standing between her and the end of her shift was one of her untroublesome regulars the door opened and Miss London-Return walked in.

She hadn't always been Miss London-Return. When Noor was growing up she was just Bina and lived in the same block of flats as Noor – but while Noor's family's flat looked onto the garden Bina's family's flat looked onto the empty plot of land which was used as a rubbish dump. But then one day Bina announced her family was moving to London where all her uncles and cousins were already living so that her parents could help out with the family business. Family business? They were all dhobis, washing underwear for the English who only used paper and not water when cleaning themselves. Everyone in the block of flats – even those like Noor who hadn't been born at the time – knew that when Bina's uncles had first started their 'laundrette' in London Bina's father had proudly borrowed a VCR from one of his officer workers and set up a television in the window of the ground floor flat so that everyone could gather in the garden and watch a movie about Pakistanis going to London and prospering in the same business. To this day no one had told Bina exactly what the movie was all about but every so often the older ones in the building would mention it and everyone would say 'Tauba tauba', and touch their ears but they'd also start laughing immediately afterwards.

'I'll do myself – don't want too much,' Miss London-Return said, sitting on the chair, without a hello or a salaam-alaik. She always said that – as if Noor went around putting 'too much' on anyone's face.

For the first few years after Bina's family left several people in the building kept in touch with them, but gradually even the Eid cards stopped. Then one day Noor's oldest sister turned on one of the music channels and there she was – only now she wasn't Bina but VJ Ruby! Ruby? Her name wasn't even Rubina, it was just Bina. And what was that accent coming out of her mouth?

'What kind of place is this Inglistan?' Noor's grandmother said, when the family and neighbours were all called to gather around and watch VJ Ruby in her tight tight shirt and jeans. 'All our boys there become suicide bombers and all our girls become fast. Look at her, Miss London-Return.' The nickname didn't just stick in the family but, because the woman on the second floor wrote for the entertainment section of one of the evening papers, it became known throughout the country.

'This is the shirt you were wearing at the reception last month, no? So you got the pomegranate juice stain out? I knew you would.'

Miss London-Return said nothing in response, and merely dabbed more foundation onto her face and chose the wrong shade of lipstick. She might pretend she was some born and bred foreigner who went to the same school as Posh Spice from the age of four, and she might have said 'you must have confused me with someone else' to Noor when they first met in the make-up room, but Noor was going to make sure that she knew that Noor knew she was just a dhobi's daughter.

Why pretend? That's what Noor wanted to know. But

Miss London-Return, she was always pretending. Ever since she had got this job as talk-show host on Kyoon TV the tight shirts and jeans had vanished and long-sleeved kameezes with trouser-shalwars took their place. Her first day on the set, when everyone was sceptical about VJ Ruby taking the coveted place vacated by Reema Askari who had gone off to Chicago to marry a green card holder, she had totally won over more than half the Kyoon staff when she responded to the request for a sound check by placing a dupata on her head and intoning 'Bismillah-ir-Rehman-ir-Rahim.' Then she put a hand to her chest and said, 'Neckline OK? Sure? Sure? Please make sure?' so that the man in charge of checking that female wardrobes passed the censor board had to take a measuring tape and run it from the base of her throat to her neckline. He held up the tape as if it was a scorecard and announced 'Pass! With flying colours!' and everyone in the studio applauded, except Noor who had sneaked in to watch and saw how Miss London-Return used the distraction – (oh and everyone was distracted watching the tape held in the man's strong hand slowly go from her neck down her chest) – to tug the dupata off her head.

'So what are you going to do next?' Miss London-Return asked. It was the first time she had ever directed a question at Noor.

'You mean this evening?'

Miss London-Return laughed in a way that was completely different from the encouraging way she laughed at the guests on her show. 'No, silly, I mean you can't want to be a make-up girl your whole life?'

Make-up girl? She was a make-up artist! But she could smile, knowing the comment only showed how her remark about the pomegranate stain had stung.

'No, this is only until I get married. I'm already twenty-two, yaar, how much longer am I going to be a single working girl for?'

Miss London-Return was, of course, twenty-four.

The polite knock on the door – two short, gentle raps – told Noor that her regular 3pm appointment had arrived. All day she'd been switching between MTV and Kyoon TV (she wasn't really interested in most of Kyoon's shows, but she liked to see how her clients looked on-camera) but now she moved to the Islam Channel, to save the Maulana the trouble of having to ask her to do so.

He entered, smelling freshly of rose-water as always, his white shalwar-kameez gleaming and uncreased. The first time she'd felt bold enough to speak to him she suggested that Allah's light was so strong in him that it made even his clothes gleam and he'd smiled and said no, actually, it was the brand of washing soap his wife used.

'Maulana Sahib,' Miss London-Return said. 'I'm a huge fan. What you said on your show yesterday about keeping our intentions pure – too right! If more people listened to you this country would be sorted.'

Sorted into what? The Maulana was obviously as confused as Noor, and also clearly annoyed by the suggestion that his viewing figures were low. Noor was pleased to see that her old neighbour had completely failed to say the right thing. The truth was, she seemed much better at knowing how to do that with the 'inside beards' – the ones who wandered around clean-shaven, in their jeans and fake designer sunglasses but in their hearts were little fundos – than with a man of genuine piety like the Maulana.

Without anything other than a gesture of vague acknowledgment to Miss London-Return, the Maulana glanced up at the television and nodded his thanks to Noor for having switched to the Islam Channel. She didn't see why he always wanted to watch the show from which he'd been fired, but he insisted and, to be honest, she thoroughly enjoyed

'Answers' herself – far more than she enjoyed the Maulana's very dull fifteen-minute segment on Kyoon TV, during which he interpreted and explained different verses from the Qur'an; everyone knew he had been brought on board in order to appease a particular investor who objected to the fashion programme hosted by the gay designer, and the talk show with the model-turned-actress who crossed and uncrossed her legs in that suggestive manner.

The Maulana sat back in his chair and closed his eyes. Noor dipped a comb in a glass of mineral water and ran it through his beard. On the TV, the two maulanas – Longbeard and Shortbeard, Noor referred to them in her mind – who dispensed often contradictory advice on personal issues greeted their viewers and reminded them that if they used A-One Mobile to call in it would cost less than any other mobile carrier or landline.

'I don't use A-One mobile,' Noor said to please the Maulana before switching on the hairdryer and drowning out the first caller's question.

Everyone at Kyoon knew the real story behind his expulsion from the Islam channel, thanks to one of the drivers who used to work there. Shortbeard and the Maulana had been hosting 'Answers' for a little over a year, disagreeing with each other every week on even the smallest matter, when a man called during Ramzan to ask if the ban on intercourse during the hours of fasting meant he was also forbidden to kiss his wife.

The Maulana had said that Islam never forbids affection within a marriage, under any circumstances, so if the kiss is merely affectionate there is no barrier against it. But it is important to ensure that the kiss does not cause 'excitement', because that will break the fast.

But Shortbeard had turned to him with a look of incredulity. Ensure the kiss does not cause excitement, he said, mimicking the Maulana's slightly high-pitched voice. How can a man ensure such a thing? No, no, of course a man cannot kiss his wife while fasting. It is too easy to fall into a state of excitement. And then he paused and added, '...except for those who are entirely certain that they cannot easily get excited. For them, it is allowed.' And then he glanced, just for a moment, at the Maulana.

Well, it was clear to everyone watching – the driver insisted – exactly what he was trying to say about the Maulana. Particularly after that high-pitched impersonation, exaggerated just enough to make the Maulana's voice sound girl-like. What choice did the Maulana have but to tell the producers that either Shortbeard would have to go, or he would?

Noor switched off the hair-dryer and the Maulana patted his beard approvingly. She knew how to smooth out its natural wiriness with a skilled addition of product. By now, Longbeard and Shortbeard had already moved on to the next call.

The caller was a woman, neither old nor young from the sound of her voice, who identified herself as Shireen.

'What can we help you with, Shireen Bibi?' Shortbeard asked, as the Maulana tipped back his head and closed his eyes so that Noor could apply foundation and eye-liner, and just a little lipstick to fill out the thin lines of his mouth which otherwise, the producer insisted, made him look disapproving. She saw Miss London-Return look in her direction, and she felt certain that if she looked up they would share a smile. But that would be disrespectful of the Maulana, who at least had the graciousness to leave the make-up business to the make-up artist and not pretend he could do a better job himself.

'I have just returned from Hajj,' Shireen said.

Longbeard and Shortbeard – and the Maulana – all quickly uttered congratulations and invoked blessings, and Noor felt compelled to join in. Miss London-Return said nothing.

'You must not call yourself Shireen,' Shortbeard said. 'You are now Hajjan Shireen.'

There was a pause from Shireen that went on too long.

'She's regretting this call,' Miss London-Return said, with the satisfaction of one who understands the minds of callers, even though she'd only been hosting the call-in chat show for two weeks.

'Something... disturbing happened,' Shireen said, and Noor, who was about to sweep the eye-liner brush across the Maulana's lower lid, paused.

With his eyes still closed, the Maulana said, 'You can listen just as well while attending to my eyes.'

'Sorry,' Noor mumbled, and touched the brush to his eyelid.

'I couldn't see the Ka'aba.'

The Maulana's eyes jerked open and a line of black smeared across his cheek.

'What do you mean?' Shortbeard said.

'I couldn't see it. I was with my husband, and his two sisters, and they all said, what a glorious sight, doesn't it fill your heart with light. Don't you feel Allah's presence? And I said, what are you talking about? What is it you're looking at? The Ka'aba of course, they replied. What else is anyone looking at? At first I thought, well, my eyes are weaker than theirs and I haven't had my prescription checked in a long time, perhaps I need to walk a few steps closer to see what is visible to the rest of them...'

While the Maulana was staring with concentration at the TV Noor quickly spat onto a tissue and wiped away the smear of eyeliner from his cheek. So what did this woman expect? That just because she went on Hajj, her eyesight should become perfect? She glanced across at Miss London-Return who was looking at the screen with an expression of disgust. Well, so they shared an opinion. Noor, too, wished Shireen would hang up so they could move on to the next call. It was the questions about family relationships she most enjoyed – how to deal with a feud between your wife and mother, what to say when a decent boy with a good career proposes for your younger daughter when your older daughter is still unmarried, what to do when your husband is posted to America and tells you you'll have to bring up your children there for the next few years.

Noor had once heard the henna-haired controller complain that these TV shows were giving too much power to the maulanas, making them fulfil the advisory roles that belonged by rights to the elders of a family. The role of the maulana is simple, he said. To officiate at weddings and funerals, and to teach children how to recite the Qur'an in Arabic so their lips can form the sacred words. But giving advice? What mad idea was this to think they should give advice? Noor listened sympathetically and nodded as he said this, but couldn't help thinking that if the elders of her own family hosted 'Answers' it would be very boring.

Shireen was still talking. 'We drew closer and closer to the Ka'aba, and still I couldn't see it. But something had taken possession of my brain – I can't explain it, but I could feel it, something inside my brain.'

This was beginning to get interesting. The Maulana nodded his head thoughtfully and pinched his lips between thumb and forefinger. Thank god she hadn't applied the lipstick yet.

'Go on,' Longbeard said.

Miss London-Return had an uncapped tube of eyeliner in her hand but instead of applying it she was simply holding onto it, looking at Longbeard with an expression identical to the one with which she'd stared at Noor in their childhood days when she came across her encouraging one of the younger girls in the block of flats to eat some animal droppings which she insisted were chocolate.

'Finally when my husband and sisters-in-law insisted it was looming up in front of us, so close they could almost touch it, I finally saw it. But only for a moment.'

'What do you mean only for a moment?' Shortbeard said

in a voice so stern it made Noor frightened for the woman calling in. She had done something terrible – Shortbeard's voice left no doubt about it.

'It wavered. One moment there, then gone. Again, one moment there, then gone. And then, whatever it was that had taken hold of my brain, it made me faint. Right there, just ten feet away from the Ka'aba, I fainted. Please tell me, what does it mean?'

There was a long pause that followed, in which time Shortbeard and Longbeard exchanged a glance filled with knowledge, Longbeard shaking his head. Noor found herself executing a rapid series of tongue-against-roof-of-mouth clicks, to show she was treating the situation with the gravity it deserved.

Longbeard said something in Arabic.

'Understand, Shireen?' Shortbeard thundered, and a whimpered 'no' was his answer. 'Do you understand any language other than Urdu?'

'English.'

'Why do you understand English, and not Arabic?'

'Because the Arabs didn't rule over Pakistan for a hundred years, you idiot, and because Arabic isn't the language of the internet.' With that Miss London-Return stood up, threw the eye-liner – uncapped! – onto the table and stormed out. A spray of black liquid speckled the mirror.

Ohhhh! Noor thought. She glanced over at the Maulana, but he was saying nothing. Oh! Oh. She had a point.

'Let's not get distracted.' Longbeard placed a restraining hand on Shortbeard's arm. 'Listen closely, Shireen. The verse from the Qur'an which I just quoted said: Allah has placed a seal on their heart and hearing, and on their eyes is a veil. A grievous punishment awaits them!'

'On their eyes is a veil!' Shortbeard echoed.

'I know that verse,' Shireen said. 'It's about the infidels. I'm not an infidel.'

'ON THEIR EYES IS A VEIL!'

The Maulana was looking down at his fingernails and pushing back the cuticles to accentuate his half-moons.

'What have you done? What sin have you committed which made you unfit to see the Holy Place?'

'Me? I haven't done anything. I'm telling you, something took possession of my brain. I think it was some kind of djinn. How do I make sure it's gone? I haven't felt it since they carried me back to my tent that afternoon and I drank a glass of Aab-e-Zamzam, so perhaps the Sacred Water drove it out, but I need to be sure. So all I'm asking is, what prayers do I say to expel it?'

'A djinn took possession of you while you were performing Hajj? A djinn has the power to cloak the Ka'aba? Woman, what blasphemy is this? Do you think the djinns don't acknowledge the sacredness of the most sacred of places in the universe?'

'You stood before the Ka'aba, and you did not see it.' Shortbeard's tone was flat, his voice suddenly quiet.

His words reverberated through the room. Noor was overcome with the awfulness of what he'd just said. She tried to imagine how it might feel to be among hundreds of thousands of people looking at the Ka'aba and knowing you were the only one who was denied a glimpse of the Holy Place. It was too sickening to comprehend. It quenches every thirst that has burnt inside you your entire life, her neighbour had once told her when he returned from Hajj and she asked him what it was like to stand before the Ka'aba. So just imagine being surrounded by a multitude who are having their thirst quenched while you're standing in their midst aware of nothing but the burning.

'You know he used to be an actor on PTV many years ago,' the Maulana said, gesturing at Shortbeard. 'Not very good.'

What did that have to do with anything? Noor wondered if

someone had sealed up the Maulana's hearing – he seemed so unaware of the gravity of what was unfolding on the television just above their heads.

'Tell us what sin you've committed!

Are you an apostate?

Do you perform black magic?

Have you burnt a Qur'an?

Are you an adulteress?

Do you tempt the pious into sin?'

'Enough! Enough!' Shireen said. 'None of that. Nothing like that. I'm an ordinary woman. I'm married, I have two children, I say my prayers, I keep my fasts, I'm honest, I'm modest, I give to the poor every Eid, big and small.'

'But you've still committed some terrible sin. Tell us what it is?'

'I haven't.'

'Why else would Allah place a veil on your eyes in front of the Ka'aba? What did you do that even His great mercy could not forgive? Remember, He is All-Knowing.'

'But then he knows something that I don't!'

'Eye-liner,' the Maulana said to Noor.

Noor looked blankly at him. Shireen wasn't lying. She could hear it in her voice. But Longbeard and Shortbeard must be right. In that place where the infirm felt strength return, where the weary of heart felt lightness infuse their spirit, who ever heard of someone losing, rather than gaining, sight? Was it possible to commit a sin of such magnitude it excluded you from Allah's grace... and not know it?

'Are you all right? Can I get you some water?'

Water? What could water do! Noor wasn't always modest, she wasn't always honest, she didn't give to the poor, she only prayed during Ramzan, and sometimes during Ramzan she pretended her menstrual cycle was continuing on longer than it really was just in order to have one or two extra days off from fasting. She had always thought these were small sins, but who was she to judge? What was the line that separated the sins that could be erased from the Ledger by a night of prayer from the ones that marked you as beyond redemption? She had always thought that line would be deep and wide and clear to anyone who considered leaping across it. But Shortbeard had asked 'do you tempt the pious into sin' as if that was enough on its own to make Allah place a veil over your sight and plan a grievous punishment for you. And Noor sometimes tempted, she knew that. Did she ask if they were pious before she walked past them, her hips swaying just a little, her eyes teasing...? No, never. In fact, she'd even once seen the henna-haired controller look at her in that particular way of tempted men, and it did nothing to stop her from stepping over, instead of around, the car-barrier which the young guard pretended to raise between her legs.

'Where is your husband? Call your husband to the phone!'

'Yes, yes. He's outside, just across the road. Wait – I'll call him. He'll tell you I've done nothing wrong.'

A minute or so passed, in which time Longbeard and Shortbeard said nothing, but only shook their heads and lifted their hands in prayer, and Noor received a text message from one of her cousins telling her she HAD TO tune in to the Islam channel NOW, while the Maulana sighed exaggeratedly and started to apply lipstick to his own mouth.

Finally a man's voice came on the phone. 'Yes?'

'You are Shireen's husband?' Shortbeard's voice echoed strangely. Shireen must have turned on the television in her house.

'I am. I'm Haji Ali. She just told me what you've said to her. Now listen – I don't know what happened to her in front of the Ka'aba, but I know she's a good woman, a good Muslim.'

'Are you saying you know more than the Almighty does? That He was wrong? Is that what you're saying?'

'Of course that's not what I'm saying. I'm saying...'

'What?'

'*You're* wrong.'

The Maulana let out a high-pitched cackle. Noor glanced at him. He'd applied the lipstick in a manner that made his lips even thinner than normal.

Shortbeard leaned back, his hands folded together. 'Really? We'll see.' He turned to the cameras. 'Viewers, some one among you may know what crime Shireen, wife of Haji Ali, has committed. Our second phone line is waiting for your call. The number is at the bottom of the screen.'

'And remember,' said Longbeard, 'Use A-One Mobile for the lowest charges.'

Almost immediately, a female caller's voice was piped into the studio. 'I know what she's done.'

'Khala, what are you doing?' Haji Ali said. 'Please don't listen to her. She's my mother's oldest sister. Her mind stopped working some years ago.'

'Quiet, Haji Ali. Please, caller, continue.'

'She does black magic.'

Noor shook her head in disbelief. She knew what mother's older sisters were like. Her own eldest Khala spent all day looking out of her window, just waiting to catch her nieces in some bad behaviour. Fortunately, the nieces knew exactly that area of ground onto which their Khala's balcony looked out.

'You've seen her perform black magic?' Longbeard asked.

'I've seen *her*. That's enough. My nephew could have married any girl. Why would he choose someone with such dark dark skin if she hadn't done black magic on him?'

Noor smiled at her own fair-skinned reflection in the mirror.

'I'm afraid that isn't proof enough,' Longbeard said.

'But if she is doing black magic she's not going to do it in full view of her family,' Shortbeard cut in. 'Such things are done in secret. The only witness is Allah.'

'But we can't just . . .' Longbeard started.

'There was a veil before her eyes. In front of the Ka'aba.' Shortbeard turned to Longbeard. 'Are you saying there is any doubt about her guilt, regardless of whether or not we know what she's guilty of?'

'Don't give in, don't give in,' the Maulana urged.

'Of course I'm not saying that.'

The Maulana sighed. 'Coward.'

'Haji Ali,' Shortbeard said softly. 'You know what you have to do now.'

'What does he have to do, Maulana Sahib?' Noor asked, her voice surprising her with its trembling quality.

'Improve viewer figures so that A-One Mobile renews its advertising.'

There was no time to respond to this ridiculous remark because Shortbeard pointed his finger in the direction of the camera and said, 'Haji Ali, divorce her.'

'Ya Allah!' the Maulana bellowed, and Noor texted her cousin to say '!!!!!'

'Say it three times!' Shortbeard instructed. 'I divorce you, I divorce you, I divorce you.'

'For the sake of your children!'

'For the sake of your soul!'

There was a long beeping sound. Haji Ali had hung up.

Shortbeard turned to Longbeard. 'It's a good thing we have Caller ID.' He called out to someone in the studio: 'Phone them back!'

Longbeard tilted his head in a way that Noor recognised as indicating someone was speaking to him through his earpiece.

'We're transitioning to a new phone system,' he said. 'Caller ID is temporarily disabled.'

Shortbeard made a gesture of disbelief. 'Viewers, it's time for an ad break. Please stay tuned.'

Maulana switched off the television. He always switched it off just after Shortbeard instructed the viewers to 'stay tuned.'

'But. . . why couldn't she see the Ka'aba?' Noor wanted to know. 'Switch it back on. Maybe she'll call back.'

The Maulana looked at her as if she was something very small and far from grace.

'What? I just want to know what she did wrong.'

'You should worry more about yourself and less about others.'

'Me? Why? I don't have anything to worry about?'

The Maulana looked ruefully in the mirror - his incomplete eye make-up, his thin, smeared lips. 'Do you think Shireen worried until the day she stood in front of the Ka'aba?'

They didn't say another word to each other as she finished readying him for the camera.

A few minutes later she was on her way to the bus-stop. She hadn't even glanced at the Pathan guard as she exited the building, and she'd stepped around instead of over the car-barrier. The mid-afternoon sun was hot overhead, and there were no trees for shade on this long road, just one office building after another, and the slightly fishy whiff from the harbour. Cars drove past, full of men. She didn't look in their direction. Tomorrow she would wear a looser shalwar-kameez with longer sleeves. Perhaps she'd cover her head with a dupata. Yes, why not?

She turned the corner just in time to see her bus pull out from the bus stop. All this thinking had slowed her down. She trudged over to the stop, and waited. So hot. The pavement itself burning through the thin soles of her shoes. And her head was beginning to ache.

She was shifting from one foot to the other when a car rolled to a stop beside her and Miss London-Return rolled down the driver side window.

'Lift?'

Noor shook her head.

'No? What's wrong? You look upset.'

'Why do you care?'

'I don't really. Just curious.'

Something about the answer made Noor get into the passenger seat.

'They tried to get that woman's husband to divorce her.'

'Well, that's men for you, isn't it? I swear, it's impossible around here to work out what you need to do to just be left alone. What's your secret?'

'My secret?'

'You come and go, you're single, professional, attractive, you talk to all the men without anyone calling you a slut, you hop on and off public transport, don't cover yourself in a shuttle-cock or hide in your own private car with windows up and doors locked – you just. . . you're just you. Living your life, and being left alone to do it. Like a miracle.'

Like a miracle! Noor was silent for a few moments as this new version of herself sank in. She could feel it expanding her lungs, pulling her back up straight. Then she understood, and it made her feel a little bit sad, but not too much.

'I manage it by not being noticed a lot. You'll never have that.'

The two women smiled at each other, both acknowledging the mingled defeat and triumph of their lives.

'Thanks for the lift. I'll direct you to my home.'

'I know where you live, silly,' Bina said.

Imtiaz Dharker

The Right Word

The right word

The right word
Outside the door,
lurking in the shadows,
is a terrorist.

Is that the wrong description?
Outside that door,
taking shelter in the shadows,
is a freedom-fighter.

I haven't got this right.
Outside, waiting in the shadows,
is a hostile militant.

Are words no more
than waving, wavering flags?
Outside your door,

watchful in the shadows,
is a guerrilla warrior.

God help me.
Outside, defying every shadow,
stands a martyr.
I saw his face.

No words can help me now.
Just outside the door,
lost in shadows,
is a child who looks like mine.

One word for you.
Outside my door,
his hand too steady,
his eyes too hard
is a boy who looks like your son, too.

I open the door.
Come in, I say.
Come in and eat with us.

The child steps in
and carefully, at my door,
takes off his shoes.

Aixa at the Alhambra

It wasn't the man. It was the garden
that seduced me. The breeze
glanced off the white mountains
and blew secret messages to me.

I looked at the pomegranate blossoms
and they blushed.
The leaves on all the myrtles
shivered when I passed
and I suspected they felt what I felt.

Out of deep shade, oranges winked at me.
Flowers turned to look. I felt adored.

Then the cypresses began to speak to me.
I came to understand
every lift of leaf and turn of limb
quite intimately.

Birds came to my fingers and nibbled there.

The sun stretched over
groves of lemon trees.
The sun suggested I'd be cooler
if I took off one veil,
then another.

Fountains whispered.
From the pool in the courtyard,
the water invited me in.
Don't be afraid, the water said,
it won't hurt a bit,

and gently, gently slipped over my body,
water fingers, water tongues.

Then I ate a pomegranate.
The juice stained my skin.

This garden is out of control now.
A garden rampant.
It grew and grew and grew right into me.

Today a bee stung my mouth.

I know you think it was him.
But it was just the garden, all along.

Never trust the daffodils

He distrusts daffodils
and is especially wary of crocuses.
Traitors of hope, he says,
they promise spring
and callously deceive you
into optimism.

He has learned to question
the ordinariness of things,
never to stroll in
with his hands in his pockets,
whistling.

He has learned the hard way
to be pleasantly surprised
when the frost forgets
to come up from behind and bite.

He turns his back, moves on.

Green shoots break through
the winter clods of earth.
Against his better judgement,
his shoulders feel
the touch of spring.

I need

I need *sarson da saag*,
nothing else will satisfy me,

and hot *makki di roti*
with butter melting over it.

I need to eat bacon and eggs
and the petals off a rose, one by one.

My greed has no nationality.
I need my mother's chicken *salan*.

I want her to break the *roti*
scoop up the gravy

and keep putting it in my mouth
until my hunger's done.

I need to run
out to my father's land

and sit in the *ganna* field
where I can hear the sugar growing,

juice rushing up through the stem
to reach my waiting mouth.

I need to tear the outer skin
and crunch the sugar-veins.

I am hungry to be the woman
watching the young man

bathing at the well,
water running down his back,

streaming down the length
of his black, black hair.

I need to crack walnuts with my teeth
and eat their brains.

I need to take a train
to somewhere, and get off

at platforms I don't know
to drink sweet milky tea

steaming in the early morning
out of earthen *khullars*.

I need to go to Crawford Market
through the piles of fruit

and buy a whole sack
of ripe mangoes

to suck and suck
till nothing is left but dry seeds.

I need you to come back.

Triska Hamid

Islamic Tinder

A civil servant, an international lawyer and an entrepreneur walk into a café. All three of these individuals are attractive young Muslim women from London. The only joke is the state of their love lives.

Like many other successful Muslim women in the West, they're single, struggling to find a man to marry and increasingly treated as failures by their communities as they creep over into their thirties.

'Muslim men are a disappointment,' says Amira, the lawyer. 'They're not as accomplished and there tend to be fewer men of the same academic level and career success. I've yet to meet someone from my community who has been better than me.'

This may seem like an arrogant statement to make, but it's a sentiment shared by many. Muslim men, these women claim, want a submissive wife, one who will not compete with them and make them feel emasculated.

'We've evolved into this new genre of women that our communities haven't adapted to,' says Noura, the civil servant.

Those belonging to this genre are mostly Oxbridge or Ivy League-educated (or both), independent (too independent for arranged marriages), financially stable and well-travelled, but also religious. The delicate balance they've cultivated between their Muslim and Western identities is a source of personal pride, but in reality they're pariahs – far too outspoken for their ethnic side and too prudish and traditional for the West.

They're minorities within a minority, shunned by most of the men in their own communities 'who fall under two categories: losers who want their mums to find them a wife, or idiots who spend their time sleeping with white women before marrying someone from a village in the mother country', says Ayesha, the entrepreneur. 'A few years ago I fell in love with a guy I thought was perfect for me. He ended up marrying his cousin from back home. Now, most of the decent Muslim guys I meet are either married or still in the closet. It's hopeless.'

Arranged marriages are archaic and offensive to these women and those like them. Matrimonial websites such as singlemuslim.com or shaadi.com are seen as a last resort, or, more commonly, a sign of utter desperation.

'I don't want a husband for the sake of being married; I want someone who I can connect with and then marry,' says Noura.

Dating is increasingly regarded as the one viable solution, but these women are amateurs. Despite their successes in education and work, their love life isn't quite as developed. They're virgins, abstaining from the world of dating and boyfriends in their teenage years and early twenties and shunning 'inappropriate relations' with men so as to avoid any scandal or gossip that would tarnish their reputation. They've kept life halal.

'I would date, to a degree,' says Amira. 'It is the chance to exercise agency and autonomy and choice, but only within the religious boundaries of abstinence and modesty.'

Unfortunately, finding compatible men to date is still an issue. Segregation is customary, particularly among Muslims of Asian heritage, limiting the amount of interaction between the two sexes.

But a few tech-savvy Muslim entrepreneurs have recently stepped up to offer a solution – Muslim-centric versions of Tinder.

Instead of casual dates and one-night stands, the imaginatively named Minder, Muzmatch and Salaam Swipe focus on marriage. All three apps were launched back in 2015 and have steadily gained traction across the UK and the US.

'No one asks, "Where are the good Muslim women?"' says Haroon Mokhtarzada, founder of Minder. 'The app has been developed with the point of view of the women – they are the ones who are faced with the problem.'

As with Tinder, users can swipe right if they like the look of someone and can start talking if they're a match. Unlike Tinder, the apps allow users to filter results according to race, ethnicity and level of religiosity.

These apps have caused a bit of a buzz among the community of young Muslim professionals in Britain. Muzmatch, launched by Manchester-based Shahzad Younas, boasts 50,000 live profiles on his app – two-thirds of which are men. He says the app has helped facilitate more than 300 marriages in the past year, but our high-achieving girls haven't had much success.

While all three have tried the apps and have met guys through them, they have ended up swiping left more than right. Some men are quite explicit in wanting to meet a woman with a British passport, some have dedicated their picture galleries to their gym bodies while others have yet to learn their angles.

'I've met a few nice guys on Muzmatch but many have felt intimidated when they find out where I was educated and what I do for a living,' says Ayesha.

Shahzad admits that despite the number of men on the app, the women tend to be more educated, and the older women (i.e. over thirty years old) have a more difficult time getting matches.

The problem is not so much with the apps themselves, it's the quality of Muslim men available. Fewer Muslim men have graduated from Oxbridge and Ivy-League universities compared to women, and those that have end up marrying outside their academic community.

'It's as if our being their academic equals means we must be inadequate wives and mothers,' says Noura.

All of these girls have been called 'intimidating' and 'outspoken' by their Muslim male counterparts, simply for being themselves. Their accomplishments usually leave men feeling emasculated, they say.

'It's still going to take Muslim men a couple more generations to catch up and realise that girls like us want love, not money,' says Ayesha.

Note: Names of the women have been changed.

Nafeesa Hamid

This Body Is Woman

1.   This body is woman. Grown woman. Doesn't wet the bed any more, Mother, woman. Ready to baby, woman. Will not fetch her brother his drink, woman. This body is touched like woman. This mouth is all woman with its no-thank-you's and dryness and gobbled-up greed dreams of wanting to write about being woman.

2.   She says I am Sex tonight. Really, you are, can't you see? Looking down I see my breasts plump and hairless flung out of my sex dress like sleeping strays. I know this body is woman. This body is power.

3.   My little sister is ten. When we leave the house my mother says to her 'Put on a longer dress!' My father says 'where is her scarf? Where is your scarf, girl?' They are getting her ready to woman when her woman body is still curled up foetal, like, let me sleep for ever. Her belly and cheeks plump with Girl, with reading Jaqueline Wilson and experimenting with the neon-pink free lipstick from *Girl Magazine*; she is not ready to woman, with her cherry-peaked breastlets, her ears unpierced,

unsexed. I do not want her to ever woman. She is already looking for the power of woman and my parents are already telling
her that woman needs no power. Has no power. When she was
born they were telling me the same. My body is no place for
man, no place for me to woman like woman, like *real* woman.

Let me start again. I am ten and my only wish is to have a
sister, preferably older, her name would be Nabeela. I'm jealous
enough not to see the shift in my parents' hands – no one
flinches in the house any more. I read *Girl magazine*, wish
for a sister to teach me how to experiment with neon pink.
She is becoming woman. Perhaps she is already more woman
than I was at ten. We will never show Mother our unfurling
pomegranate bodies. Hold on to your seeds, girls.

My little sister is already looking for the power of woman
and I'm grinding down the idea right in front of her eyes,
telling her to keep running, keep running, we just gotta keep
running, kid. Our bodies are no place for us.

4. This body is man crawling out through woman. Woman
clawing to find man in her fat, not-quite-size-10 thighs and
36 I'm-not-quite-sure-I'm-a-B-cup-any more breasts. This is
woman. It is all over me like a disease I was born to catch for
offending Mother Nature – the Devil – in another life. The
way my hands burn when I touch this woman body of mine
is a sure sign woman is a work of the devil – is ill. My woman
body is ill. I am all striped thighs, arms slashed deep enough for
woman to feel like *something,* like more than woman herself,
more than woman alone, lonely woman. This woman body
has been made to love, to withstand man with all his hate, to
soften him and his offspring. There is too much love in this
woman body.

5.   This woman body once tried to piss standing up. She wondered how the boys did it without bending their legs. She thought they just dealt with the discomfort. She dealt with the cold, broken seat and her naked, baby legs instead.

6.   This woman body burned, like ghost pepper spice at your throat, when her Mother found the porn stash. She did not explain that she just wanted to know what she was growing up to be and whether or not her vagina was normal. She did not know vaginas from pussies back then.

7.   This woman body was once stupid enough to have got herself kidnapped, and then stupid enough to ask her mother why Khayam was allowed out but she weren't. Her mother said it was because she was stupid enough to have got herself kidnapped. This woman body did not flinch with regret when she told her mother she blamed *her*. This woman body did not cry after the slap. She just stood red, in her woman skin, unmoved. Unapologetic.

8.   This woman body cannot remember the first time she saw dick. Maybe she does and won't say. Maybe she can't say because it was dark at the back of his car and his blue jeans *were* unzipped, but the flesh he flashed was probably just leg. She closed her eyes anyway.

9.   This woman body once liked the way her hair sat beneath a hijab. She decided to wear her new-found pride on the first day of year 7. Her father said 'Of course she should!' Her mother said 'Of course you will – you're a woman now. Don't you know?'

10. This woman body does not know how to twirl her frigid hips to music, only to men who will ask no questions about

who she is, what she likes, where she was born, whom to and what she loves. Maybe she likes feeling like a dirty rag, like the dirtiest pages of those dirty, western magazines her father used to sell.

11. This woman body does not need to be told it is clean, pure, virgin-smothered silk. Because it does not feel like it ever has been and so she asks God to forgive the misfortune of being Woman that He blessed her with.

12. Do you know this woman body, the body of this woman with her lubricated secrets hand-wrapped for the nine-year -old girl who lay in the back seat of his car begging to see her mother? Do you know this woman body that does not fit into size small salwar kameez any more, only into the baggyness of her western world? She struts into gay bars these days, all sexed up with sizzling flesh and dark eyes, her glittered body dripping away fat in the heat. She leans at the bar and smiles, thinking God can't see her being woman here. This woman body decided not to think about God tonight

13. This woman body sees this other woman in a way where she can only wonder how the hell she does it so damn well. Woman feels in a way she is not supposed to. She watches her rock back in her chair and enjoys her wide smile and her grey, gold-tipped eyes for a moment that's not long enough to feel guilty about later. She hears those click-clack, clattering keys speed and slow in time with her mind, she feels the last few letters being pushed down, feels herself being pushed, pushed, pushed… and then she knows to stop feeling like this, because click-clack clattering keys are even against her ears as she sleeps. This ain't right, she thinks; imagine she knew. She'd hate you.

14. Be woman. Bent woman. Be man. Bent man. Arched back woman, with your leg hooked up on to his lap, at his crotch. Woman, like sexy woman, like black lace thong and matching bra with velvet kisses on each strap, woman. Watch Him as it womans down your shoulders, uncapping your woman breasts, left perfectly rounded, leaving him wanting you to woman more and more and faster and faster. You are loving being woman like this! God is nowhere to be seen.

15. This woman body does not cry. Not even when it's left alone, in dark double-bed alone. Not even into the back of man. Not into the sloped neck holes of other woman; she womans too much and womans too close and it makes this woman body feel shame, feel alone in her sole, womanly shame. She watches *Coronation Street* and waits for them to tell her when to cry. She watches depressing films about kids with no homes, and kids on the run and beaten wives and abused kids and starving kids and lost men and she waits for them all to tell her when to cry. She womans like this woman body of mine. I cry about the state of my woman. About being too woman, too little woman. Too much. Try and remember how to cry.

16. Woman like no one is watching you. Woman like no one is ever going to read you or watch you up on mic. Woman like you have everything to say.

17. When you had me up against that tree in Ward End Park, our noses melting into each other in the cold, my blazer crumpled on the frozen grass, the cold air from your mouth forcing me back into the tree, and you jokingly threatened to rape me, I knew then I was not ready to woman.

18. This woman wonders when she'll become a good human. How long?

19. I want to woman like this other woman. And that other woman. And that one. And that one. And that one too.

20. When you knifed him, you did not feel like woman, did you? You did not feel you could ever baby with all this Man inside of you. This was not how to woman.

21. My mind is all woman. It is uneasy. My doctor tells me part of my woman is ill. I don't want to woman any more, I tell him. He nods without looking at me, his glasses do not budge from the tip of his nose as he continues to take notes. He asks how long. I say since my mother birthed me and named me Woman. He asks how long. I say too long. He says the new tablets will help me woman again.

22. This woman mouth collapses when I ask her what's wrong. Woman does not know why she cannot woman properly in this world. Why she stops fighting like woman at least once a day, puts the weight of woman down and says 'Fuck off. Go find someone else to carry you. I don't want to do this any more.'

23. Woman stands in summer storm with a hi-vis jacket and no umbrella. Rain drops are catching and collecting on the front peak of her hijab, then dropping and sliding down the sides of her face to form a beard at her chin. The playground is empty today, silent – the trees are still and watching with breath held at woman who is bent double under the monkey bars, knees folded against chest, crunching her foiled fate against her unholy body, ready to be unwomaned.

24. Being woman is like being this McDonald's Happy Meal balloon in the middle of the four-lane traffic. It wants to get hit, doesn't get hit, changes its mind and bobs away to the edge,

at the railing, wondering how to get itself out of this mess. She is stood playing footsy with her own feet at the edge of the four-lane, wondering how to get out of this mess.

25. Woman like no one is watching. Woman like no one is ever going to read you. You have everything to say.

26. Are you? I don't know. Do you think you are? I'm just in love with her though. It's just her. It's just her. It's just her. Just her.

27. Pulled up from
the pavement on
Cotterills Lane crying,
by strange women
with kind faces.
They tell girl
it'll be okay.
Inside their home,
her mother tumbles
through door, falls
at feet – pink
scarf throttling around
her neck – unashamed.
Eyes bloodshot sockets,
noosed hair hitting
against her face.
Father follows slow
and soft like
he has seen
and known death.
He tries to
smile, but cries
over head of

Girl instead. He
fathers. They speak
with strange voices.
Girl does not
listen, but hears.

28. When you birthed me did you smile? Or did you remember chores instead? Did you hug me that night, the next day,
a week later in secret, in the middle of the wheat fields, at the
side of your bed, in the middle of the night? Your first girl. So
much trouble to be born with this girl.

29. My Aunty says they used to woman by shoving pencils
down sides of sofas, passing discreet notes like chewing gum
in class or selling fags in the corridor at lunch time, all because
my grandfather preferred silence. I watch him now; still sat in
the same corner of the room, still watching, through older eyes,
still conducting silence in this room, all these years later as me
and my siblings sit twiddling our thumbs in front of him on
Eid day.

30. (Mum's spicy chicken wings)
Rumble. Grumble. Rumble.
Splash, stroke, thrust
and rest.
I'm thinking she probably doesn't want to touch me;
she looks at me with blank eyes,
too full with other thoughts
for me to be seen;
she's bored of this lifetime routine.
Chop, cut, chop, chop, cut –
I don't bleed.
Spark – it doesn't light up so she tries again.

Spark.
Flame. Thump, sizzle.
My skin tightens around my body,
anaemic legs burn in the heat.
My insides loosen up.
She swings me on to my back,
prods her finger down my spine;
grunts.
I'm picked out, well-browned; just how they like me.
Brown on the outside, pink on the inside.
A cultural mish-mash.

The boys rush to greet me,
grab me by my leg and slap me
on to their plates;
my sweat already congealing their fingers.
The boys like me;
their eyes all bright and empty like hers.

They tear off my crackling coat
and dig teeth into my flesh
which falls off at ease.
The boys like me
when I'm well-browned
and have stopped sizzling
and am silent.

31. (Defence: after Jamila Woods)
Girl touch turn
Everyone soft
Her sultry temptress
Medusa or siren/
Her red lips
Suspicious/ boy

Frisks every bump
Girl in bed
Be like girl
On street corner or
Girl on dance table
Girl brush teeth spit
Even her spit

Say sex.
Her a walking
Casualty/ whole
Body asking for it
Predator/ sinner

31. (How men are made)
Perhaps this is how men are made
Perhaps he was more man than fist
Perhaps she closed her eyes
Instead of glaring straight into his eyes like an insolent child
Perhaps she sunk her knuckles into the leathery skin of sofa
Rather than at his face.

The Ramadan calendar is four years out of date and still no
one will take it down.

In a freeze frame we all look bored more than we do tense,
more than we do scared, more than we do broken.

In awkward angles (because this is a freeze frame)
we are waiting for him to kick her balloon belly,
waiting for her to scream, fall to floor, crawl towards door,
waiting for someone to stop them,
waiting to wake up,
waiting for God to answer all the prayers we made up

in the madness,
waiting for my brother to cry but still look like man
in his five-year-old skin
because real men watch, they don't walk
waiting for her to bruise,
keep asking for more – her mouth wide awake in this frame
she will not shut up
waiting for him to tell us he is a hard-working man,
hard-working father and husband –
he is not monster.
Perhaps this is how men are made.

This is an extract taken from a stage show in development.

Ahdaf Soueif

Mezzaterra

Holland Park. He came towards me through the crowd in the drawing room of the grand house that I'd never been in before and have never been in since. 'Come,' he said, 'I'll show you the menagerie.' That was twenty-five years ago. I have, in some sense, been examining the menagerie ever since.

I had thought it made no difference where one lived: Cairo, London, what was a four-and-a-half-hour flight? We were citizens of the world and the world was fast becoming more connected. I saw the difficulty only in terms of the personal life: on the one hand, how much would I miss my family, my friends, the sun, the food, the – life? On the other, what was life worth without this miraculous new love?

We married in 1981. But I did not move to London permanently until 1984 when our first child was born.

I shared, then, in the general life of the country that had become my other home. I supported Spurs, kept an eye on house prices, formed political opinions and found that whatever view I might hold about Thatcher or Europe or the NHS, I was bound to find it expressed somewhere in the common discourse of the mainstream media. Where I felt myself out of step was when this discourse had anything to do with Egypt, the Arabs or Islam. I had become used to what was at the time unequivocal support for Israel in the British media, but it troubled me that in almost every book, article, film, TV or radio programme that claimed to be about the part of the world that I came from I could never recognise myself or anyone I knew. I was constantly coming face to face with distortions of my reality.

I reasoned that this must be the experience of every 'alien' everywhere and that it shouldn't be taken personally. But it was a constant irritant – and world geo-politics meant that interest in where I came from was growing. Lebanon was suffering the tail end of both the Israeli invasion and its own civil war (which was the direct result of the troubles in Palestine). Afghanistan became the crucible in which thousands of disaffected, young – mainly Arab – Muslim men were being transformed into a fighting force pitted against the USSR. Then the Soviet Union imploded. The Gulf War came and with it the imposition of sanctions on Iraq, the basing of US troops in the Arabian peninsula and talk of a New World Order. In the run up to the Gulf War, Israelis and Palestinians were summoned to negotiations in Spain and Norway and the world applauded while a perceptive few foresaw the mess for which the Oslo accords laid the ground plan.

It was impossible – apart from a few notable exceptions – to find in the media of the West coherent interpretations of all this that did justice to the people of the region and their history. If the New World Order was a mechanism to control the Arab and Muslim worlds then I felt that the media of the West was complicit in it; for they always represented those worlds in terms that excused or even invited the imposition of control.

Was this misrepresentation reciprocal? If I were an American or British person living in Egypt, and if I knew Arabic well enough to read the mainstream Arabic press, would I constantly be brought up short by skewed accounts of my history and culture? Would I switch on the television to find a doom-laden voice intoning about how the Celts worshipped the massive stones placed on Salisbury Plain by astral beings? Would I switch on my car radio and hear an account of yet another outbreak of 'Christian paedophilia', with a background theme of church bells and Christmas carols? Would I wander into the movies and come face to face with an evil American character bent on destroying the 'third' world so the cinema audience cheers when the Arab hero kills him? I have to say the answer is a resounding no. Where the Arab media is interested in the West it tends to focus on what the West is producing today: policies, technology and art, for example – particularly as those connect to the Arab world. The Arab media has complete access to English and other European languages and to the world's news agencies. Interpretive or analytic essays are mostly by writers who read the European and American press and have experience of the West. The informed Arab public does not view the West as one monolithic unit; it is aware of dissent, of the fact that people often do not agree with policy, of the role of the judiciary. Above all, an Arab assumes that a Westerner is, at heart, very much like her – or him. Many times I have heard Palestinian village women, when speaking of the Israeli soldiers who torment them, ask 'Does his mother know he's doing this?'

Living in London, I know that I am not alone in the experience of alienation; there are hundreds of thousands of us: people with an Arab or a Muslim background living in the West and doing daily double-takes when faced with their reflection in a western mirror. I felt upset and angered by the misrepresentations I encountered constantly and I felt grateful when a clear-eyed truth was spoken about us. And then again, who was 'us'?

I went to school in London briefly when I was thirteen. Mayfield Comprehensive in Putney. There, the white girls thought I was white (or thought I was close enough to white to want to be thought of as white) and the black girls thought I was black (or close enough to black to make identifying with the whites suspect). But that did not mean I could associate freely where I chose; it meant that I had to make a choice and stick with it. And whichever group I opted for I would be despised by the other. After three months I refused to go to school. Thinking about it now, I see this as my first serious exposure to the 'with us or against us' mentality; the mentality that forces you to self-identify as one thing despite your certain knowledge that you are a bit of this and a bit of that.

Growing up Egyptian in the Sixties meant growing up Muslim / Christian / Egyptian / Arab / African / Mediterranean / Non-aligned / Socialist but happy with 'Patriotic Capitalism'. On top of that, if you were urban/professional the chances were that you spoke English and/or French and danced to the Stones as readily as to Abdel Halim. In Cairo on any one night you could go see an Arabic, English, French, Italian or Russian film. We were modern and experimental. We believed in Art and Science. We cared passionately for Freedom and Social Justice. We saw ourselves as occupying a ground common to both Arab and western culture, Russian culture was in there too, and Indian, and a lot of South America. The question of identity as something that needed to be defined and defended did not occupy us. We were not looking inward at ourselves but outward at the world. We knew who we were. Or thought we did. In fact I never came across the Arabic word for identity, huwiyyah, until long after I was no longer living full-time in Egypt. Looking back, I imagine our Sixties identity as a spacious meeting point, a common ground with avenues into the rich hinterlands of many traditions.

This territory, this ground valued precisely for being a

meeting-point for many cultures and traditions – let's call it 'Mezzaterra' – was not invented or discovered by my generation. But we were the first to be born into it, to inhabit it as of right. It was a territory imagined, created even, by Arab thinkers and reformers, starting in the middle of the Nineteenth Century when Muhammad Ali Pasha of Egypt first sent students to the West and they came back inspired by the best of what they saw on offer. Generations of Arabs protected it through the dark time of colonialism. My parents' generation are still around to tell how they held on to their admiration for the thought and discipline of the West, its literature and music, while working for an end to the West's occupation of their lands. My mother, for example, who had fallen in love with the literature of Britain at school, and who could not be appointed to teach it at Cairo University until the British had left, did not consider that rejecting British imperialism involved rejecting English literature. She might say that true appreciation and enjoyment of English literature is not possible unless you are free of British colonialism and can engage with the culture on an equal footing. This is the stance that Edward Said speaks of when he describes how 'what distinguished the great liberationist cultural movements that stood against western imperialism was that they wanted liberation within the same universe of discourse inhabited by western culture.'

They believed this was possible because they recognised an affinity between the best of western and the best of Arab culture. ... Generations of Arab Mezzaterrans had, I guess, believed what western culture said of itself: that its values were universalist, democratic and humane. They believed that once you peeled off military and political dominance, the world so revealed would be one where everyone could engage freely in the exchange of ideas, art forms, technologies. This was the world that my generation believed we had inherited:

a fertile land; an area of overlap, where one culture shaded into the other, where echoes and reflections added depth and perspective, where differences were interesting rather than threatening because foregrounded against a backdrop of affinities.

The rewards of inhabiting the Mezzaterra are enormous. At its best it endows each thing, at the same moment, with the shine of the new, the patina of the old; the language, the people, the landscape, the food of one culture constantly reflected off the other. This is not a process of comparison, not a 'which is better than which' project but rather at once a distillation and an enrichment of each thing, each idea. It means, for example, that you are both on the inside and the outside of language, that within each culture your stance cannot help but be both critical and empathetic.

But as the Eighties rolled into the Nineties the political direction the world was taking seemed to undermine every aspect of this identity. Our open and hospitable mezzaterra was under attack from all sides.

Personally, I find the situation so grave that in the last four years I have written hardly anything which does not have direct bearing on it. The common ground, after all, is the only home that I – and those whom I love – can inhabit.

As components of my mezzaterra have hardened, as some have sought to invade and grab territory and others have thrown up barricades, I have seen my space shrink and felt the ground beneath my feet tremble. Tectonic plates shift into new positions and what was once an open and level plain twists into a jagged, treacherous land. But in today's world a separatist option does not exist; a version of this common ground is where we all, finally, must live if we are to live at all. And yet the loudest voices are the ones that deny its very existence, that trumpet a 'clash of civilisations'. My non-fiction, then, from the second half of the Eighties, through the Nineties, rather than celebrating Mezzaterra, became a defence of it, an attempt to demonstrate its existence.

It was as though a simple-mindedness descended on the media when it reported on matters to do with Arabs, Islam and, in particular, Palestine. No, it's a bit deeper than that: it is that the media attributes simple and immediate motivation to Arabs and Muslims as though they were all one-celled creatures. Watching the news on the BBC or CNN on the one hand and Al Jazeera on the other was like seeing reports from two different planets.

As we now know, the New World Order announced at the beginning of the Nineties was – by the beginning of the new millenium – mutating into the Project for the New American Century. An extreme strand of American ideology deemed the omens propitious for America's 'manifest destiny' to be actualised: it was time for America to dominate the world. The key to this would be strategic control of geography and of the main energy resource of the planet: oil. Dominance in central Asia and the Arab world would both control the oil and prevent those parts of the world from forming alliances with China or Russia.

But the US could not underwrite Israeli policies and ambitions in the region and at the same time be regarded by the Arab people as a friend. The Palestinian issue was largely at the heart of this, but so also was the Arab reading of Israel's desire to become the local superpower. Apart from the questions over the Syrian Golan Heights, the Lebanese Shab'a Farms and the never-quite-renounced expansionist 'Eretz Israel' idea, Israel's footprint was to be found in many issues critical to the wellbeing of its neighbours such as the debate over Egypt's share of Nile water, the surreptitious introduction of GM crops into the region's agriculture or the growing drug trade. America, therefore (and this is before September 11, 2001), could not seek to secure its interests in the region through a positive or mutually beneficial relationship with the Arabs.

This is never spelt out by the American media for the American public: that the discord between the Arab world and the USA is entirely to do with Israel.

The events of September 11, 2001 played straight into what would appear to be the Neo-con dream scenario. With the collapse of the Soviet Union the US no longer needed the Islamist fighters it had helped to create in Afghanistan. In fact they had become a nuisance since the US refused to cede to the demand of their leader, its one-time ally, Osama bin Laden, that American troops be pulled out of Saudi Arabia. The political groundwork for dealing with the Arab world in terms of pure power had been laid by the Neo-cons who were now in central positions in government. The ideological framework for a confrontation with 'Islam' had been fashioned by Samuel Huntington and his followers out of the anti-Islamic discourse prevalent since Khomeini's revolution in Iran. Now the War on Terror was declared. Israeli politicians leapt to declare common cause with America, or rather to declare that their cause had always been the war on terror and now, at last, America had joined them.

It was now possible to move the conflict from the political into the metaphysical sphere: a conflict with an enemy so nebulous as to be found anywhere where resistance to American or Israeli policies might lurk.

To date, the effect of American policies on the Arab world has been the complete opposite of their stated aims. In Palestine America defined itself as the 'honest broker' between the Palestinians and Israelis and proceeded to place matters in the hands of US Special Envoys almost every one of whom was a graduate of AIPAC. Today, after more than thirty years of an American-sponsored 'peace process', thousands of Palestinians and hundreds of Israelis have been murdered, Jerusalem is encircled by illegal settlements, the West Bank is decimated, an Apartheid barrier is in the process of construction and the President of the US has taken it upon himself to absolve Israel of any obligation to conform to past agreements, to international law or to the declared will of the world. Gaza and Rafah are seeing killings and demolitions of homes on a scale unparalleled since 1948.

And still the media burble on about the 'peace process' and bringing 'democracy' to the Arabs. Almost 300 years ago Giambattista Vico pointed out that the first symptom of the barbarisation of thought is the corruption of language. The media has a clear duty here: the US administration and the British government should be made to define very precisely what they mean by 'sovereignty', 'democracy', 'freedom', 'stability', 'peace' and 'terrorism'. These people are not vague idealists; they are lawyers and businessmen, they know all about fine print and defining terms. They run democratically elected governments answerable to the people and their representatives. The media should demand that they spell out the fine print in their pronouncements to their electorates. We could even limit the question and ask what do the British and the American governments mean by these terms in the context of their dealings with the Arab world?

And since the western media is now blithely using Arabic words it would be useful if they could demonstrate their understanding of those too. They can start with 'jihad', 'fatwa' and 'shaheed', all of which are far more layered and subtle than you would guess if you just came across them in English.

The whole question of Islam and the West needs to be examined honestly. The current pieties that say 'we know so little of each other' or, in the words of Lord Carey, the ex-Archbishop of Canterbury, 'we must get rid of the deep hatred we have for each other', may be well-intentioned but they rest on untrue premises and are not helpful. The huge populations of Arab Christians and the Christians who live in Muslim countries know a great deal about Muslims and there is no evidence that they 'hate' them. In fact Arab Christians have fought side by side with their Muslim compatriots against the Crusaders and against the Western colonialists of more recent times. And Muslims are very well informed about Christians. Eastern Christians have been their compatriots, neighbours and friends for fourteen centuries. And Muslims have had to learn about western Christians if only because the West has been the dominant power in Muslim lives for the last 200 years.

As for hatred, a 'secular' Muslim cannot, by definition, hate a Christian or a Jew on the grounds of religion. A 'believing' Muslim cannot hate a Christian or a Jew because of who they are since Islam is clear that Muslims must live in fellowship with people 'of the Book'. There is, though, an important difference between Christians and Muslims in terms of belief. Since Islam came after Christianity and Judaism and saw itself as a continuation of their traditions, it is part of the faith of a Muslim to believe in Christ, Moses and the prophets of the Old and New Testaments. This is stated in the Qur'an and it is not open to choice. A believing Christian or Jew, on the other hand, can choose whether or not to believe that Muhammad was a prophet and, therefore, whether Islam too came from the God of Christianity and Judaism.

A linked and recurrent theme is to claim that Arabs use Israel and the West as an alibi, an excuse for their passivity, that they should get on with fixing their lives, with developing. Here it is essential to differentiate between the Arabs and their rulers. The rulers will do nothing because their only interest is to remain in power. They have failed in their primary task of protecting their nations' sovereignty and steering their countries' resources towards providing the people with a decent life. Their positions are now so precarious that they dare not move one way for fear that their people's anger will finally unseat them, and they dare not move the other way for fear of offending America. As for the people, they are doing plenty. First they are surviving – by the skin of their teeth. The poor are poorer then they have ever been. The middle classes are often running two jobs just to make a living: civil servants are driving taxis, lawyers are working as car park attendants, graduates are working on food stalls. Even so, local NGOs challenge governments on human rights, on trade union laws, on constitutional reforms. Citizens challenge government officers on corruption. They take cases to court and they win. Artists paint and musicians sing. Newspapers are full of analysis and debate. And this against a background of arbitrary detention, of torture, not just in prisons, but in police stations. Protests are organised despite the thousands of armed security forces the state puts on the streets. And despite the sullying of these terms, people still campaign for democracy and freedom.

It should be said that representation in the western media is not high among the priorities of my friends in Egypt and other Arab countries. Nor should it be. But for those of us who live in the West this fashioning of an image that is so at variance with the truth is very troubling. As Jean Genet observed in *Un captif amoureux*, the mask of the image can be used to manipulate reality to sinister ends. And while it would not be correct to attribute malign motives to the media in general, it is not unreasonable to feel that by promoting a picture of the Arab world that is essentially passive, primitive and hopeless, a picture that hardly ever depicts Arabs as agents of action (except for terrorists and suicide bombers), the media validates the politicians' dreams of domination.

It has become commonplace to say that the world has never known such dangerous times. It's possibly true. The givens we live with at the moment are well-rehearsed: the absence of a world power alternative to that of the United States, the US's umbilical links with the global ambitions of capital and corporatism, and the reach and power of contemporary weapons.

I would add to these that the identification (despite the efforts at blurring) of Islam as 'the enemy' is particularly dangerous. When the West identified the USSR as 'the enemy' it had to construct 'the Evil Empire' from scratch. But with Islam, the idealogues and propagandists of the West need only revive old colonialist and orientalist ideas of Islam as an inherently fanatical, violent ideological system that rejects modernity. They can play to deep-seated fears and prejudices with roots stretching back into the Middle Ages. When, at the height of the Troubles the IRA launched a bombing campaign on the mainland, the suggestion that this was a manifestation of 'Catholic fanaticism' was a marginal one. However repellent their bombing of civilians it had to be regarded and dealt with as a politically motivated act. A similar reaction was afforded the African National Congress's bombing campaign – no reasonable person suggested that this was 'black fanaticism'. From 1970 to 2000 the United States has been directly implicated in creating and nurturing Islamist groups to counter secular national liberation movements in Palestine and other Arab countries. It, and the Arab regimes, have succeeded in pushing most political opposition into the cloak of Islamism. Now that the most militant of the Islamist extremists, whose lands are the 'objects' of Western policies, are no longer content for the battles to be fought exclusively on their home ground and have brought a sample of the carnage into the territory of the West we hear a ready-made discourse on 'nihilistic Islamic fanatics' who are on the rampage because they hate the democracy, freedom and prosperity of the West. One does not have to condone the murder of civilians to admit the political demands behind it. In fact denying the existence of these political demands guarantees the continuation and escalation of the conflict and the deaths of yet more innocents.

The role of Israel here needs to be clearly acknowledged, for Israel has always predicated its value to the West on the premise that there is an unresolvable conflict between the West and the Muslim hordes. Today, allied to the American Christian right, its role is to exaggerate and escalate the conflict.

A bleak, bleak picture. And yet there is still hope. Hope lies in a unity of conscience between the people of the world for whom this phrase itself carries any meaning. We have seen this conscience in action in the demonstrations that swept the planet before the invasion of Iraq, in the anger of Americans and Europeans at the pictures coming out of Abu Ghraib prison in Iraq, in the brave stand of the Israelis refusing to serve the Occupation, and in the private citizens from every part of the world who have tried – and some have paid with their lives – to stand between the Palestinians and their destruction. We see it every day in the writings of the brave and dogged few in the mainstream media and in the tireless work of the alternative and fringe media. It expresses itself in a myriad grass-roots movements that have coalesced into a world-wide effort to influence and modify the course of global capitalism.

For all these voices, these consciences, to be effective, however, western democracies have to live up to their own values. It is shameful that on questions of international politics there is so little to choose between the governing parties and the opposition in the US and Britain. Democracy presupposes vigorous opposition on matters of national importance; it also presupposes a free and informed media which sees its task as informing the electorate of the facts. The current attacks on civil rights on both sides of the Atlantic, the drive to place security concerns before every other concern, the attempts to tamper with education and the law to serve a political agenda remind me of nothing so much as the activities of the ruling regimes in the Arab world for the last several decades.

The question of Palestine is of paramount importance not

just because of humanitarian concerns about the plight of the Palestinians. It matters that, now, in full view of the world and in utter defiance of the mechanisms the international community has put into place to regulate disputes between nations, a favoured state can commit vast illegal acts of brutality and be allowed to gain by them. If the world allows Israel to steal the West Bank and Jerusalem and to deny the history of the people it dispossessed in 1948 and 1967 then the world will have admitted it is a lawless place, and the world will suffer the consequences of this admission. The question of Palestine is also where the influence of the USA on world affairs is most sharply in focus. If there is no just solution to the Palestinian problem, if the ordinary citizens of Palestine and Israel are not permitted the conditions which would allow them to live their daily lives in a human way, then the influence of the world's only superpower will be proved to be irredeemably malign.

Globalisation is happening. It is driven by economics, economic ideology and communications. But does this have to entail the economic, political, cultural annexation of chunks of the world by whoever is the most powerful at any given moment? Surely that is the path to constant conflict, to grief and misery.

There is another way, and that is to inhabit and broaden the common ground. This is the ground where everybody is welcome, the ground we need to defend and to expand. It is to Mezzaterra that every responsible person on this planet now needs to migrate. And it is there that we need to make our stand.

This is an extract from the Preface to Mezattera, *2004.*

Seema Begum

Uomini Cadranno

Tick Tock Tick Tock. 4 seconds. A person is going to die.
1, 2, 100, 500, 1000, 1 million.
Just one weapon devouring souls, good, evil, does it matter?
Tick Tock Tick Tock. 4 seconds. A person is going to die.

Tell me who is the king of mass murder,
the devil who writes the list of people who will die but at the
wrong time?
Tell me if in this endless cold, endless storm,
endless torture, endless war, endless genocide,
a sweet beauty will blossom from the seeds of this endless cold,
endless storm,
endless torture, endless war, endless genocide.
Tell me if men are the true seeds of greatness, the brains of the
body,
the strength of life, the ones who possess natural intelligence?
Then tell me, oh great man bound for greatness, why do the
innocent suffer the fate of the guilty?

Tick Tock Tick Tock. 4 seconds. A person is going to die.

And within this midst of darkness,
there are flowers desperate to bloom, pure and spirited.
But they are weak. They are fragile. They are a mistake because
they are girls.
You men in power have the audacity to prevent a woman from
achieving great ambitions.
How are you able to say 'I foresaw her fatal outcome' yet you're
not aware of her potential?
Tell me, will her humanity cause her country to crush
the way bombs crunch up cities,
spill innocent blood and break bodies?
The news of a baby girl reaches the father.
The news of a daughter born into the family.
The shame, how can the father bear the shame?
Cradles his anger in his heart but the anger is endless.
The shame is endless.
Closes his eyes, closes his thoughts, closes his mind, closes his
heart to the world.
Because the shame is endless.
'Oh my daughter, mistake of my life, use your seduction skills,
use your beauty,
weave a spell and charm a man into bearing sons, sons who
will bring us prosperity.
Wrap your beauty and fragile humbleness around men
and you might just be forgiven for being you.'

Tick Tock Tick Tock. 4 seconds. A person is going to die.

Tell me, what must I do?
I'm told to dream but am limited,
must have manners and be disciplined,
can't have an ambition and stay committed,
being higher than a man is prohibited,
sit neatly be quiet and not spirited,

get married and stay typical.
The art of a woman is no excuse to limit her potential.
Don't tell me I need a man to be complete.
Don't tell me marriage is the purpose of my life.
Oh man of my life, must I stand before you with a beautiful gown and lower my gaze?
Must I stand under the great sky in solitude and silence and curtsy before you?

No. I'm a girl who'll save endless lives, bring endless happiness, inspire endless people,
and protect endless innocents, be a shield to endless people,
challenge endless stereotypes and be a leader with endless humanity.
If men don't understand the significance of women
Uomini Cadranno –
men will fall and ladies, we will rise.

Tick Tock Tick Tock. 4 seconds. A person is going to survive.

Editor's Note: I met Seema Begum in 2016 when I facilitated a poetry workshop at Central Foundation Girls' School in East London. This was for the Poetry Society's SLAMbassadors project, which encourages teenagers to write and perform poems about identity. The workshop culminated in an award ceremony and showcase. The class were one of the most engaged I've ever taught and their feelings regarding freedom, social justice and equality were palpable and inspiring. Seema, who was in Year 9 at the time, and was just fourteen years old, wrote the above poem as a response to the question, 'Who am I?'

Leila Aboulela

The Insider

Author's Note

My play is linked to a new dramatisation of *The Outsider*, to celebrate the centenary of Albert Camus. The instinctive, visceral Arab response to this classic set in Algeria is not 'Where are the Arab characters?' because they actually do exist and they are central to the plot. But the thing is that they have no names. They are never ever named. So in *The Insider* I gave them not only one name but two. Fatima and Fifi, Yusuf and Joseph – their original Arab name and a French version that they made up when they moved from the village to Algiers. Their cultural anxiety and their dual identity is a contemporary concern and one that I see often around me. This duality got me thinking in terms of the past and the present and I wanted to give a feminine, flouncy perspective in contrast to the masculinity of *The Outsider*. But there are still parallels between Fatima and Meursault, the protagonist of *The Outsider*. Her senses respond to clothes – specifically French fashion – as Meursault's responds to nature. She is an outsider too, a prostitute in a conservative society. And at a certain point both of them find themselves alone in a confined darkness.

But Fatima is also an insider because she is not a stranger to herself and because, through loving her brother, she eventually connects to a higher form of spiritual Love.

One of my favourite novels is *Wide Sargasso Sea* by Jean Rhys in which she tells the story of the first Mrs Rochester, Bertha Mason, the mad women in the attic of Charlotte Brontë's classic *Jane Eyre*. *Wide Sargasso Sea* fills in the Creole, Caribbean world of Bertha Mason which Charlotte Brontë could not have had access to. The mad woman in the attic becomes a woman with a country and a family, her own complexities and voice. This is what *The Insider* does by extruding a slice of Camus's novel. So 'Raymond's mistress' and her brother 'The Arab' become main characters who have their own side to the story and exist well beyond it.

Editor's Note: This play was originally written and produced for radio. It has been slightly edited for this print version. The characters of the play tell their stories in two different, yet resonantly similar, times – now and during the Algerian Revolution. They interweave, often within the same scenes, and it is up to the director and creative team making the play to decide how best to present this on stage.

Characters

FATIMA
FIFI (Fatima as a young woman)
JOSEPH (Fifi/Fatima's brother)
YUSUF (Fatima's grandson, a security guard)
PAUL (a tenant in the building where Yusuf works)
RAYMOND (Fifi/Fatima's ex-lover/pimp)
POLICEMAN
HAMMAM ATTENDANT
REVOLUTIONARY
VENDOR

1. The Beach (THEN)

FATIMA: He knew about the clothes. We walked along the beach and practised saying: *jupe, blouson, chemise, combinaison*…

FIFI: …*combinaison, chandail, chiffon*…

JOSEPH: …*pantalon, smoking, veste.* That's what I need, a blue *pantalon* and a *veste* like a sailor's, please.

FIFI: And a *beret* to match.

JOSEPH: *(Laughing)* You would. And a pair of *espadrilles.*

FATIMA: Everything Joseph wanted I got him and what wouldn't I do for a new dress?

FIFI: …lime green and *décolletée*, the skirt all in *dentelle.* Walk and turn heads, walk slowly and quickly turn heads.

JOSEPH: Fifi!

FIFI: *(Distracted)* Mmm?

Fifi shrieks as Joseph splashes her, and they chase up the beach.

FATIMA: There was a wooden *chalet* which Joseph and I admired. We would stop walking and gaze at it until a strong wave soaked our ankles. We imagined ourselves inside it, living so close to the sea, spending whole days at the *plage.* Now when I remember the French in Algeria, I think of this beach house and I understand them better. I imagine myself rich enough to own a holiday *chalet.* It is an extension of my belongings but not my permanent city flat. As I go about my everyday life, the *chalet* remains in my mind as empty, waiting for my visit. I know, in a vague sort of way that there are people who live on the beach all year, but to me they are only a background. They might be watching, or having their own lives, but they are not important.

2. A Flat in Algiers (NOW)

A telephone rings.

FATIMA: Yusuf!

The telephone continues to ring.

FATIMA: *(exasperated)* Yusuf! Yusuf!!!

Fatima hauls herself to her feet and starts to walk slowly to the phone, muttering under her breath. As she approaches the telephone it goes to answering machine.

PAUL: *(on the machine)* It's Paul. Paul Sintès. Have you changed your mobile? I've been trying all day. Listen, I'm back from Paris. If you were at your post this morning, you could have helped with the luggage. And the lift still hasn't been fixed, so… so what's new. Anyway… call me, Joe. Okay?

The machine beeps.

FATIMA: Sintès.

FIFI: Raymond Sintès?

FATIMA: No, he said Paul. It must be a wrong number.

FIFI: No, it's for Yusuf. He's calling him Joe instead.

FATIMA: Why not? I used to be Fifi myself.

FIFI: Fatima has too many syllables. Fatima sounds backward. Fatima is not *chic*.

FATIMA: I refused my mother's veils and went out in the street wearing lipstick.

FIFI: I turned heads and not only Arab ones.

FATIMA: Then came nationalism and war.

FIFI: Veils, you said. Talk about clothes, not war. Don't pretend you've forgotten… the first *décolleté* he ripped open, that *robe* with the stain you couldn't wash out…

FATIMA: War made us rough and bitter. But we got our aspirations. Our young speak Arabic now instead of French. We have our own tyrants and they are not French.

FIFI: The city. It started with the city. Dreaming of it, hanging on every word that was said about Algiers. I didn't belong in this village. Every fortune teller said so.

FATIMA: The city showed up in Mother's coffee cup. In every single cup. A black whorl of grains, delicate rectangles for buildings, the sea clean bare china without a single speck of coffee.

FIFI: She would suck it with a slurping sound, put the saucer on top then flip it over. Wait a bit. Let those fine grains settle into tiny maps, a route to the sea, a woman flaunting her hair wild all the way to the rim of the cup. And me holding my breath.

FATIMA: To hear what you wanted to hear. Nonsense. These fortune tellers peddled with people's hopes. They read their eyes.

FIFI: What did they read in Mama's eyes?

FATIMA: That her young daughter was becoming a handful. Too much breast and thigh for the stepfather to handle.

FIFI: He hated me.

FATIMA: He hated the temptation. Day in, day out. Making a mockery of his sense of honour.

FIFI: And I wanted Algiers.

FATIMA: And that's what the fortune teller said. She said: 'Fatima won't be with us for long. She will go far and up'.

FIFI: Far and up. Marriage was the first thing that came to Mama's mind.

FATIMA: Yes, she would have approved of that. Marriage to a young lad from another village.

FIFI: I was through with villages. Our village was pushing me out. Its animal smells and early nights.

FATIMA: Ein Fakroon. Named for the hill that was shaped like a turtle. Yusuf used to go there to fly his kite, his cheeks would go red with the cold.

FIFI: Like an apple but the skin all chapped. But after…

FATIMA: Ten lashes with his belt…

FIFI: One across his cheek because he twisted…

FATIMA: Mama said we had to thank him for putting food on the table…

FIFI: Thank him for beating Yusuf? For not letting me go to school?

FATIMA: We ran away the two of us—

FIFI: Fifteen years old and ten.

FATIMA: At the end the city was even more cruel.

FIFI: But at the beginning the city was Life. Crystallised, lit up, jumping. Algiers, the buildings, the sea, the cafés, the beach and the French women… their clothes. What wouldn't I do for a new dress? The sleeves just right, the swish of the skirt, high heels and new words to learn, *jupe, blouson, chemise, combinaison…*

FATIMA: I'm remembering too much.

FIFI: …*combinaison, chandail, chiffon, corsage…* What wouldn't I do for a new dress?

4. Outdoor Balcony of Flat (NOW)

FATIMA: (*calling*) I'm out here!

YUSUF: (*bending down to kiss her on both cheeks*) Aren't you cold?

FATIMA: Not at all. Oh God, what happened to your face?

YUSUF: (*pulling a chair to join her*) That's nothing. They smashed my phone.

FATIMA: Who?

YUSUF: The police. Because the fancy madam up in the penthouse was burgled last night. She left her window open and some kid made off with her laptop and her microwave.

FATIMA: But you weren't on duty last night.

YUSUF: That's why they let me go. But I'm fired. The night shift and the day shift – all four of us are out.

FATIMA: You'll find a new job, don't worry. You look handsome in your uniform.

YUSUF: Thanks for trying to make me feel better.

FATIMA: Is that the telephone?

YUSUF: No.

FATIMA: (*standing up*) A Frenchman called you. He left a message on the answering machine. He said his name was Raymond Sintès.

YUSUF: Raymond? It must be Paul.

FATIMA: Yes... Paul, that's what he said. It's there you can hear it. He said Paul Sintès.

FIFI: Raymond, Raymond...

FATIMA: Stop.

FIFI: Oh, Raymond dressed well. Remember... straightening his tie in front of the mirror, the cigarette almost falling from his mouth. And that buckle on his belt – I used to shine it till I could see bits of my face in it. Lick it and wipe. Lick it and wipe.

FATIMA: Enough.

YUSUF: He's one of the tenants.

FATIMA: Maybe he can help you get your job back.

YUSUF: I doubt it. Grandma.

FATIMA: Yes, darling.

YUSUF: Sit down, you've just been standing, or do you want to go inside?

5. The Phone Call, Flat (NOW)

Yusuf is on the phone.

PAUL: There you are! New number.

YUSUF: Yes. Sorry.

PAUL: I heard what happened. Are you okay?

YUSUF: Yeah.

PAUL: With the police and everything?

YUSUF: It's cool. I'm home.

PAUL: Wow.

YUSUF: I'm fine.

PAUL: Joe… What can I say?

YUSUF: You could talk to them. Maybe. I mean I – I didn't know anything – I wasn't even there—

PAUL: Sure. Sure, I'll do that.

YUSUF: Really?

PAUL: Really. Of course. Can we meet?

Pause

YUSUF: Yes.

PAUL: Okay.

6. The Flat (NOW)

Fatima is watching a daytime chat show on TV.

FATIMA: I used to lie to Raymond that I had friends and that I was meeting them for coffee. He believed me.

FIFI: The brothel is not a place to make friends. Remember the fights. Remember the girl who had acid thrown in her face? Poor thing, she was no use any more.

FATIMA: We competed for the most generous men, the ones who behind Raymond's back spared us a franc or two.

FIFI: Or a *cadeau*. Remember the *cloche* hat..

FATIMA: Snug in winter..

FIFI: *Plis* on the sides, a trim of gold *brocart* all around.

FATIMA: *Chic.* I don't remember who gave it to me.

FIFI: The sweaty one…

FATIMA: They were all sweaty.

FIFI: The one with the scar all along his armpit.

FATIMA: That scar I can remember but nothing else.

FIFI: He was a sailor from Marseille. He knew a bit of Arabic.

FATIMA: I remember.

FIFI: He was easy to please, that one.

FATIMA: It was a life soaked in sin.

FIFI: It made sense. My body had a value, a use. Strip naked for the money. Lie down for a *cadeau*. Coax them. Ease their anger, release the build-up inside them…

FATIMA: As good as a commode…

FIFI: But worth it for a new dress. There is nothing like putting on a new dress. I have to close my eyes, I smell the fresh material and then my head comes out. My hair has come undone. I stand in front of the mirror and turn this way and that. I raise my arms up like a dancer. I turn sideways like a model. Oh, I could look at myself for hours.

FATIMA: Such vanity…

FIFI: Vanity? Sin? You never used those words in the old days.

FATIMA: I've changed.

FIFI: You should go on this show. You could phone in.

FATIMA: 'A Prostitute Repents?' I don't think so.

FIFI: Or, 'I Too Played My Part in the Revolution?'

FATIMA: The Revolution was the last thing on my mind. I certainly never spoke up except for that one time.

FIFI: 'I can get you into the warehouse.' I was wearing my black skirt.

FATIMA: By the time I got to those meetings, I was always in black.

7. The Kitchen (NOW)

YUSUF: Move, Grandma, let me lift this.

He lifts a bucket from the sink. Fatima closes the tap.

FATIMA: I've done the bathtub and six large bottles.

Yusuf rummages in the kitchen cabinets.

YUSUF: Here — these too.

He's taking out saucepans.

FATIMA: It's only eight hours, they said.

YUSUF: And they keep their promises, do they?

Fatima sighs, takes the pans and starts to fill them from the tap.

YUSUF: I hate coming home to no water.

FATIMA: What can we do? This is the situation the country is in. I don't know how families with five or six children are coping. It's bad enough they've got them in tiny two-bedroom apartments, then the council cut the water and the power...

YUSUF: I ran the washing machine.

FATIMA: Thank you, Yusuf. I do pray that you would find a job soon but I'm actually enjoying your company. It's like when you first came to live with me. I would tell you, 'Go down and play football with the neighbourhood children.' And you would just shake your head.

YUSUF: I was nervous.

FATIMA: But you settled in. At first you were sitting on my lap watching from the balcony the children playing football. Then one day you didn't need my lap any more. And one day, you let me take you downstairs and you stood apart just watching. Then you joined in.

YUSUF: What would I have done without you?

FATIMA: You don't need to say that.

YUSUF: But it's true. I was an orphan and you took me in.

FATIMA: You're my grandson and my responsibility.

YUSUF: I didn't even know you.

FATIMA: My daughter was ashamed of me. That's why. I don't hold it against her and you mustn't. She had the respectability I didn't have. And because people will always gossip I agreed to keep away. When she named you Yusuf it was her way of telling me that she loved me in spite of everything.

JOSEPH: It's Joseph in Algiers, don't forget. We're not villagers any more. And I am finished with begging. No more sitting on the sidewalks. No more holding out my palm and looking sad.

YUSUF: Grandma?

JOSEPH: You're right, Fifi, I need to learn a skill. I want to be a railway mechanic.

YUSUF: Sit down Grandma. You're looking pale.

Fatima heaves herself into a chair.

FATIMA: I'm fine. I'm fine. Time to make my coffee and I'll perk up, that's all.

YUSUF: I'll make it for you, sit.

Clatter as he makes the coffee.

FATIMA: You've brightened my life, you have. And one day soon, I hope, I will help you get married.

YUSUF: I'm out of a job and you're talking about marriage! When did they say the water would cut?

FATIMA: At one. So we have about … let's see…

She as she peers at her watch.

YUSUF: Ten minutes. Enough for a shower.

He heads off hurriedly.

FIFI: How can you have a shower when I just filled up the bathtub?

8. The Beach (THEN)

Fifi and Joseph are walking on the sand.

FATIMA: I paid for Joseph's apprenticeship in instalments. It included food and lodging. When he finished and earned his first wage, we went to the *plage* together. We ate grilled corn and walked on the sand.

JOSEPH: It's good, right?

FIFI: It even smells wonderful. I bet if you cook it indoors it won't taste the same.

JOSEPH: If we lived in that *chalet* you could have your morning coffee looking out at the sea. And there's a little garden at the back too, look. I want to be rich and buy one.

FIFI: They're not for us.

JOSEPH: I've been to these meetings where they say – well they're more like discussions really – they say if we want to be French citizens we shouldn't have to give up Sharia. Like we can't be us, like we don't exist.

FIFI: What meetings?

JOSEPH: I've been to three. All of us go, the railway workers, even in our overalls. A few women too. You should come.

FIFI: What use would I have for a bunch of low-paid Arabs? And you should stay away from trouble.

JOSEPH: They're my friends. One of them lent me ten francs.

FIFI: You just got paid, why are you borrowing money?

JOSEPH: I'm sorry.

FIFI: Joseph! And you didn't even buy yourself a new shirt. Look at you, all hot in your boiler suit because you've nothing else to change into.

JOSEPH: I got you a present.

FIFI: What?

JOSEPH: It's in my pocket. Guess.

FIFI: A lottery ticket.

JOSEPH: How did you—

FIFI: It's the only thing I'd wish for which could fit in your pocket. *Merci.*

JOSEPH: I hope you win.

FIFI: What else did you squander your first wage on?

JOSEPH: I bought a pocket knife. It's a beauty. Honest. Look. It's heavy. It's not cheap. And yo! Look how that blade is catching the sun.

FIFI: Alright, I get it. Put it away. It's a waste of money.

JOSEPH: *(impersonating gangster slang from a Hollywood film)* Kitten, there are goons in this city, there are hatchetmen and there are coppers ready to fill the likes of me with daylight. There are grinches and gunsels, there are those who're plenty rugged and even gents these days are wearing metal.

FIFI: So you've been to the cinema too.

JOSEPH: Yes, I have. *(in slang)* Stick 'em up, Greaseball. Or else bang. Bang.

Fifi laughs.

JOSEPH: Stick 'em up, I said.

FIFI: Okay, okay. There…

JOSEPH: *(sudden change in tone)* What's that bruise?

FIFI: Where? Oh it's nothing. That yellow dress I have, its sleeve is too tight. It must have pinched me. Ouch, let it be.

JOSEPH: Sorry.

FIFI: Forget it.

JOSEPH: Someone did this. Someone hurt you.

FIFI: Of course not.

JOSEPH: Swear to God.

FIFI: I swear.

JOSEPH: I don't believe you.

FIFI: Come on, I'll race you to the pier.

JOSEPH: No one should hurt you.

FIFI: He just stood there in his boiler suit. The knife in his hand. That funny expression on his face. Confused. Like he couldn't really and truly for the life of him understand why anyone would squeeze my arm so tight and twist it and pin it above my head.

9. Street in Algiers (NOW)

Yusuf is on his mobile phone.

YUSUF: Hello?

PAUL: Where are you? I've been sitting here like a—

YUSUF: They won't let me come up.

PAUL: Who?

YUSUF: The new guards. I'm not allowed in the building. They don't even want me hanging outside.

PAUL: Shit. So what then?

YUSUF: Did you ask them?

PAUL: Ask them what?

YUSUF: About me. Did you tell them? That I didn't know?

PAUL: Sure.

YUSUF: Because I haven't heard.

PAUL: I told them. I put in a good word for you.

YUSUF: What did they say?

PAUL: Look, can we talk about this— Where are you now?

YUSUF: If they could give me a reference, even. I don't want to— I'd rather not be doing what I'm doing.

PAUL: I understand.

YUSUF: Even for the money, you know.

PAUL: Where can we meet?

YUSUF: Uh…

PAUL: Not on the street, okay? Can I come to your place?

YUSUF: Well…

PAUL: Think of somewhere. Call me back.

YUSUF: Okay. Okay.

10.   The Flat (NOW)

Fatima is dreaming. In the dream the telephone rings a few times. The answerphone clicks on.

RAYMOND: Fifi.

Fatima sleeps.

PAUL: Fifi.

FATIMA: Yes.

RAYMOND: Come here.

FATIMA: No.

PAUL: Come to my place. I have a *cadeau* for you.

FIFI: What is it?

RAYMOND: What is it? That's more like it.

FATIMA: I won't come.

PAUL: A silver bracelet.

FIFI: *Faux?*

Paul (acting as Raymond). He is no longer on the phone, but close to her.

PAUL: No. Here, put it on, take a good look at it before I close the shutters.

FATIMA: Raymond, I'm leaving…

RAYMOND: You think I still want you. Look at you, a hag now. Smelly like a dog… What's this? (*he grabs her thigh*) like a piece of raw chicken.

FIFI: Please…

PAUL: Beg me, yes… You want it but I'll spit in your face first. (*He laughs.*)

Fatima enters another dream.

PAUL: (*as a TV presenter*) Madame, you are live now on the nation's French-speaking channel. One of the earliest attacks carried out by Algerian revolutionaries was officially recorded as an accident. Who got away with it?

FATIMA: You want to talk about crime. Is that it? The earth is heavy enough with sin. My husband died in the war. He was a soldier in the *Front de Libération Nationale*.

PAUL: I'm sorry for your loss. But if I can take you further back in time. Tell me, what was your relationship to Raymond Sintès?

End of dream.

FATIMA: He was a gangster and I was the special one he kept for himself. Not like the others. I was his Moorish pet. And I was proud of it.

FIFI: Oh how they envied me… I would wrap the sheets around me and gloat…

FATIMA: Above his bed there was a stucco angel—

FIFI: Pink and white – just staring calmly at us.

FATIMA: I took it down but he got angry. He hung it up again.

FIFI: The angel made me feel soiled. It made me feel tired.

FATIMA: You do everything with a man—

FIFI: You strip naked, you kiss his feet and let him punch you, you let him knead you and push you and kick you – he was so strong—

FATIMA: I would be covered in bruises…

FIFI: …then cigarettes and more kisses…

FATIMA: Before the next quarrel flared up. But still I don't remember his face… or why he got angry when he found something in my bag…

FIFI: It made him think I was cheating on him.

FATIMA: What was it?

FIFI: It certainly made him livid—

FATIMA: Whatever it was. What I remember clearly are the pin-up pictures in his room. My favourite was the brunette in a bathing costume—

FIFI: Her legs wide open on the sand, her mouth closed over a lolly.

FATIMA: I remember that I could beat him in cards.

FIFI: Raymond was such a sore loser.

FATIMA: You do everything with a man…

FIFI: Everything he wants and what he doesn't know he wants…

FATIMA: And then years later you don't remember his face. Nothing. Good though. Like the washing powder advertisement on television. The stains are gone and the shirt is all clean and fresh. Look at me now. I walk down the street and people see a grandma dressed decent. Two years ago I went to Makkah, I went to the house of Allah and asked Him to forgive my sins. I am not proud of what I've done. I am only content when I forget. It is better to dwell on sweet thoughts like the mint I am growing on the balcony. Or gripping stories like the TV series I watch in the evening. Or even worries like my poor grandson.

11. Living room in Algiers (NOW)

Fatima is watching television. The babble of an Arabic TV soap in the background.

YUSUF: Grandma. Grandma, put this down a little.

FATIMA: What is it?

YUSUF: I need something from you.

FATIMA: And where am I going to get it from?

YUSUF: We can pawn your bracelets till I find a job.

FATIMA: No. They're all the savings I've got.

YUSUF: For my sake.

FATIMA: No. Let's wait a bit. You went out early this morning. Any luck?

YUSUF: Nothing much. I'll be putting on a boiler suit soon instead of a uniform.

FATIMA: Nothing wrong with that. As long as it's honest work. You just have to be patient.

YUSUF: Patient, patient.

FATIMA: Is that the phone ringing?

YUSUF: Your mind is wandering.

FATIMA: Who knows? I'm all ripe for the Angel of Death but he must be fooling around with someone else.

YUSUF: You should go out more often. You haven't been to the hammam in ages. Or anywhere else.

FATIMA: You want me out of the way so that you can steal my bracelets?

YUSUF: *(getting up angrily and starting to walk away)* Now you're getting paranoid.

FIFI: You never go out?

FATIMA: I haven't gone out in months. I live like a nun.

FIFI: Even nuns go out.

FATIMA: I get fresh air from the balcony, I get exercise cleaning up the flat. I sleep-pray, eat-pray, wash-pray, cook-pray, talk to Yusuf-pray, iron-pray, scrub the dishes-pray…

FIFI: Enough. It's clear enough… It's also 'Yusuf, we've run out of gas. Yusuf, we've run out of couscous.'

FATIMA: He's an angel. Though sometimes I have my doubts.

FIFI: Is he like Joseph, soft in the head?

FATIMA: Joseph was fine. There was nothing wrong with him.

FIFI: He never asked where the money was coming from. The money for his apprenticeship.

FATIMA: He knew well enough.

FIFI: But he didn't ask.

FATIMA: I didn't want him to ask. He knew.

FIFI: But he wasn't sure.

FATIMA: It was there in the background. Something to be sensed but not spoken about. Something you would arrive at only by sitting down and really figuring it out.

FIFI: Like a difficult sum.

FATIMA: Yes, or a puzzle.

FIFI: Joseph was useless at puzzles.

FATIMA: Slow, not useless.

FIFI: I told you, he was soft in the head.

FATIMA: I remember him saying, 'When I earn a wage you won't need to work?'

FIFI: As a waitress, he meant.

FATIMA: Once he met me in town. I was walking out of a bar with Raymond.

FIFI: He had his arm around my waist.

FATIMA: He was drunk.

FIFI: I was in my black *jupe* and red *corsage*. Unsteady in my *chaussures à talon*.

FATIMA: And Joseph pretended he didn't know me. He didn't stop to say hello.

FIFI: He didn't nod. He didn't smile. He just walked past.

FATIMA: *Crétin*, Raymond said.

FIFI: Why?

FATIMA: Maybe Joseph stared at me for too long.

FIFI: I copied him. *Crétin*. I was tipsy. I wanted to cry.

FATIMA: We never spoke about it.

FIFI: Like it was too late to question it.

FATIMA: Like nothing could be done to change it. So why mention it.

FIFI: But what does the Arab brother do when his sister loses her honour?

FATIMA: 'What's that cut on your forehead?' he'd say.

12. (THEN)

JOSEPH: Fifi, what happened to your head?

FIFI: I walked into a door.

JOSEPH: You walked into a door. Who told you to walk into doors?

FIFI: No one did. Too much wine, that's it.

JOSEPH: I don't believe you, Fifi. A door.

FATIMA: Yes, love, a door. And you kissed it better for me.

FIFI: Look, when an Arab woman loses her honour, what happens?

FATIMA: Nothing good happens.

FIFI: What does her father or brother do?

FATIMA: They throw her out.

FIFI: If she's lucky.

FATIMA: They beat her up.

FIFI: Until they kill her and no one stops that shamed, heartbroken father and no one punishes that furious brother who is so driven by anger that he cannot think.

FATIMA: Joseph was different.

FIFI: But I started to goad him…

FATIMA: No.

FIFI: Remember.. I said to him…

FATIMA: No! I don't want to remember!

13. Yusef's Room (NOW)

Bedroom door opens.

FATIMA: Yusuf, wake up.

YUSUF: (*muffled*) In a bit.

FATIMA: It's one in the afternoon.

YUSUF: (*rolls over*) Leave me.

FATIMA: You're turning day into night, that's what you're doing. You're out all night smoking what you shouldn't be smoking with your friends and now you sleep in. Come on, get up.

YUSUF: Go away.

FATIMA: What's this? (*rustle of plastic bag*) These trainers are brand new. And a *blouson*!

YUSUF: *Chic*, right?

FATIMA: How are you going to pay for all this?

YUSUF: I'm getting paid soon.

FATIMA: For what?

YUSUF: Stop it. Get out of my room.

She starts walking out of the room. Closes the door behind her.
Stops dead.

FATIMA: I remember now. What Raymond found in my bag that made him furious. It was the lottery ticket.

YUSUF: (*calling out from inside the room*) Sorry, Grandma. I shouldn't snap at you.

FATIMA: Raymond saw the lottery ticket that Joseph had given me and said, 'You're cheating on me.' Then a slap and I heard zinging in my ear.

YUSUF: (*Trying harder because he hasn't had a response*) Sorry if I made you cross. Just give me a moment.

FATIMA: Then another slap. And another.

FIFI: He gathered my things and threw them out the door. I took them and ran…

14. Joseph's room (THEN)

Outside, Fifi hammers on the door. She's distressed.

FIFI: Joseph! Joseph! Open, it's me. Please…

Door opens. He looks at her. She breaks down in tears.

FATIMA: That was when he knew.

FIFI: I said to him, 'You know, don't you, what men need from women, what they pay them for? What they expect to do to a body that belongs to them?'

Joseph kicks the door, shoves a little table against the wall.

FIFI: That's all you can do? Kick things around?

JOSEPH: But I caught up with him. I followed him. I said, 'If you're really a man, you'll get off this tram.' The coward got off and started to talk to me as if I were a child. As if I was no one. 'Don't get all worked up' he said. But then he punched me and I fell down. I wished that I had my knife. He was strong and he just kept hitting me. Then he asked, 'Have you had enough?' His hand was bleeding.

15. The flat in Algiers (NOW & THEN)

YUSUF: Grandma, I've got a visitor coming.

FATIMA: What visitor?

YUSUF: Paul Sintès. Remember, he lives in the building where I used to work.

FATIMA: What's bringing him here?

YUSUF: It's nothing for you to worry about. Just stay in your room. You don't need to meet him.

FATIMA: But it doesn't make sense

JOSEPH: Fifi, no. You can't go back to him.

FIFI: Raymond is sorry. That's what his letter is about. He misses me.

YUSUF: Why don't you just go out, Grandma?

FATIMA: You want me out of the way?

YUSUF: Yes!

JOSEPH: It's wrong – what you're doing is shameful.

FIFI: Is that what your friends are teaching you? Shame and honour aren't for people like us.

JOSEPH: 'Live with dignity,' that's what I'm learning. 'Fear Allah Almighty but don't fear Poverty.'

FIFI: Shut up, Joseph.

JOSEPH: You can be more than this, I know. I can help you change. Can't you see that Allah forgives everything? If you just take the first step. He can set you free.

FIFI: I am free.

JOSEPH: Are you?

FIFI: I'm free to be whoever I choose. I don't want you to pray for me!

JOSEPH: But I do and I will because I know that your soul is soft. I know you're not happy…

FIFI: I will be when I go back to him.

JOSEPH: Will you?

FIFI: Yes.

JOSEPH: I don't believe you. Sometimes you want another life, I'm sure. Not even sometimes, often.

YUSUF: Grandma.

FATIMA: It's not right.

YUSUF: Stop telling me what to do. We could do with the money.

16. The beach (NOW)

More populated than in the past. The sounds of traffic are closer. But still the sounds of the waves are strong. Fatima walks. A vendor calls to her as she passes, slowly and breathlessly.

VENDOR: Do you want to rent a deck chair, Granny?

FATIMA: No, thank you.

VENDOR: Do you want some ice cream?

FATIMA: I'm here to walk.

VENDOR: You're not going to get very far, are you?

FATIMA: I used to run.

VENDOR: That must have been a long long time ago.

FIFI: I ran back to Raymond. The wind lifting up my skirt …

FATIMA: He was waiting for me.

17. Raymond's apartment (THEN)

They're in bed.

RAYMOND: *(Very close)* 'You're a *chienne*, Fifi. Even if you travel dozens of miles away you will come back to your *maître*.'

FATIMA: And he spat on my face.

Fifi lies quietly for a moment, then hits him with all her strength. He is surprised. Then goes for her wildly, punching and kicking, pulling her out of bed.

RAYMOND: I'll teach you to do that – I'll teach you to cheat on me.

FIFI: *(Screaming)* Not my face! Not my face!!

FATIMA: I screamed until the neighbours came out, my hair

all wild, my dress half–torn … Then someone called the police…

Shouts in the landing. A dog barks. Police run up the stairs. Commotion.

FIFI: He's a pimp! He hit me! He's a pimp, he's a pimp!

RAYMOND: Tell me, officer, isn't it against the law to call a man a pimp?

POLICEMAN: Shut your mouth.

RAYMOND: *(to Fifi)* Just you wait, I haven't finished with you yet!

POLICEMAN: Shut it, will you? Mademoiselle, I suggest that you come with me down to the station and we'll leave this gentleman to cool his heels….

FIFI: *(as she's taken away)* He calls himself a warehouse man but that's not all he does. He's a pimp. Take him and lock him up.

FATIMA: But he got off with a warning and I was left with a broken rib, my face so bruised that it chilled me to look at myself.

FIFI: …the fear of being good for nothing worried me even more than the pain.

18. Outside the local hammam (NOW)

Fatima at the entrance of the local hammam and then inside. The sounds of trickling water and other women's voices in the background. (Note: Attendant is female)

FATIMA: That's not what I was charged last time.

ATTENDANT: Inflation, Granny, everything's gone up, even the hammam.

FATIMA: I bring my own towels. I bring my own soap and loofah. It's too much.

ATTENDANT: Sorry, Granny, I'm just following orders.

FATIMA: I used to work here. For years I carried buckets of cold water.

ATTENDANT: When was that?

FATIMA: Before you were born.

ATTENDANT: Here's your change.

A group of women pass by speaking in French.

FATIMA: And what are they doing here?

ATTENDANT: Experiencing a Turkish bath is now part of every tour package.

FATIMA: I came for a bit of peace and quiet.

ATTENDANT: Don't worry. They won't stand the heat for too long. They'll be out of here before you finish your scrub.

Fatima makes her way into the hammam. Louder sounds of trickling water. A furnace blows, women shuffle around in wooden clogs. Fatima settles down and starts to scrub herself while muttering to herself.

FATIMA: My skin has gone thinner.

FIFI: I could rub myself all over with a pumice stone and not complain.

FATIMA: Now a loofah is enough… In the old days my heart, my kidneys, my bowels were deep down inside me. Now it's as if they've come up to the surface ready to complain…

ATTENDANT: *(calling out)* Are you all right there?

FATIMA: What? Yes…

ATTENDANT: *(calling out)* I'll come in a minute and give your back a scrub.

FATIMA: Stay with the tourists and their fat tips. I have nothing to give you.

ATTENDANT: *(laughs)* Just don't scare them away, Granny.

FATIMA: Scared of the naked hag, are they? I won't bite.

19. Joseph's room (THEN)

JOSEPH: They say honey is good for these cuts. Move your hair out of the way. I got the purest honey for you, see the bits of wax in it.

FIFI: It stings. The flies will get me.

JOSEPH: I will shoo them away. I will stay with you. Think happy thoughts so you can sleep. A new dress. Right? *Crêpe de chine*. Beige *crêpe de chine*? Wouldn't you like that? Or a skirt *evasée*, very ladylike, very *chic*.

FIFI: The *crêpe de chine* but not beige.

JOSEPH: Why not?

FIFI: Beige is a dull colour.

JOSEPH: What colour then?

FIFI: Oh.. Is that all you're good for – swatting flies and talking about clothes?

JOSEPH: That's how you've always talked, Fifi…

FIFI: But look at me now.

Beat

JOSEPH: Do you know the very big house next to the hammam?

FIFI: Where the garden is?

JOSEPH: One of my friends lodges there, with the family. They run the hammam. He says they always need help.

FIFI: *(Looking at him)* Are you joking?

JOSEPH: You could ask them.

FIFI: The hammam.

JOSEPH: Yes.

FIFI: *(Getting upset)* Where no one would see me, you mean?

JOSEPH: No…

FIFI: Oh, but that's what you want. Me, in a bloody smock, breaking my back—

JOSEPH: To earn an honest franc. No one would hurt you—

FIFI: It's my fine luck to have you as a protector. When I'm the one who's been looking after you.

FATIMA: I didn't tell him that. I didn't.

FIFI: I must have dozed off then. He watched over me. He couldn't sleep.

FATIMA: From the moment he saw me hurt, until that day on the beach, he never slept.

20. The Hammam (NOW)

FATIMA: Dear God Almighty, thank You for this warm water, for the breath I breathe without pain. There was a time when I was a sinner. There was a time when I was an outcast, when no respectable woman would sit next to me.

FIFI: Thrown out of the hairdressers, my hair still in rollers. Pushed off the tram because I was the Frenchman's whore.

FATIMA: Now everyone around me is too young to remember. Where have they all gone, all those people who believed they were better than me? They're ill at home, they're senile and forgetful. I've outlived most of them. Is this a sign that You have washed my sins away? You changed the world so that I could walk with my head held high. I repented and you took me back. How can I be sure? I fell in love with You. Yes, love was the sign. At first there was just the remorse but now I'm not frightened... I just want You...

FATIMA: I just want to love You and be loved by You.

ATTENDANT: (*calling out*) Stop talking to yourself, Granny, you're frightening the tourists.

FATIMA: I'm sorry. It's dark in here. I can hardly see.

ATTENDANT: Never mind. The warmth is good for your bones. I'll come and give you a scrub. Hang on. Then you can stretch out and relax on the bench.

21. Yusuf's room (NOW)

They are very close together. They are smoking. Paul inhales.

PAUL: So I've asked all the neighbours too, so they can't complain.

Yusuf laughs.

And loads of people from work, and... all around basically, all sorts... and I've got a DJ sorted. I think.

One, at least. So it should be good. We're going to party all weekend.

YUSUF: Sounds great.

PAUL: So...?

YUSUF: Oh—

Yusuf jumps up. Gets out a plastic bag.

YUSUF: Yes. Plenty here. Plenty. Smell how fresh this is.

Paul stands. Stubs out joint. Gets out cash.

PAUL: It's good stuff.

YUSUF: Only the healthiest hash for you.

PAUL: *(handing him the money)* Here.

YUSUF: This isn't—

PAUL: *(taking the bag)* Thanks, Joe.

YUSUF: This isn't what we agreed.

PAUL: It's what I'm paying.

YUSUF: But I can't – I already owe people.

PAUL: That's market rate, okay? You're lucky I came. The new night porter made me a better offer. Home delivery too. *(He slaps Yusuf's thigh proprietorially, and makes to leave.)* It's been real.

YUSUF: I'll ring you.

PAUL: I don't think so.

YUSUF: I don't mind! I can come wherever you want.

PAUL: *(leaving)* Let's not do this Joe.

YUSUF: I can get you anything. Monsieur Paul!

Paul pauses at the door.

YUSUF: My job.

PAUL: Yes, Joe.

YUSUF: Isn't there anything… you know…

PAUL: Anything I can do for you?

YUSUF: Please.

PAUL: I'll tell you what I can do.

YUSUF: Yes?

PAUL: If you come near me again, I can tell them you stole from me too.

22. (THEN)

JOSEPH: On the beach I saw Raymond in the sunlight, face to face even clearer than that day on the tram. This man's money had put food in my mouth. I stared at him. The sun on my blade pinched his eyes. He lunged at me first. I punched his forehead, and swiped at his arm. Red on his shirt, just like that, my knife didn't let me down. It was easier than I thought. I wanted to kill him but my friends held me back.

FIFI: You should have listened to them. You should have gone back to town with them.

JOSEPH: But I slipped away. I went further along the beach. I lay down on the sand near the stream and that large rock. It was too hot.

FIFI: Because you were in your boiler suit.

JOSEPH: But I was content because I had hurt Raymond. I had seen the spicy fear in his eyes. *(beat)* Fifi, I stretched out on *my* sand, *my* sweet shade and the rhythmic sound of water. I turned my head and saw the *chalet* that we liked. It's not perfect. There is a lot that's wrong with it. Bits of the wood are broken and the two front legs that are sunk in the water, they're rotten through with moss clinging to them. I could see them under the water. It needs days of work, that *chalet*, a lot of fixing to set it right. I closed my eyes and thought to myself. 'The Frenchman is afraid of you, Joseph.' I sure will have something to boast about in the next meeting.

FIFI: Silly boy.

JOSEPH: I'm a hero, Fifi.

23. The hammam (NOW)

FATIMA: I never spoke to him again.

ATTENDANT: Granny?

FATIMA: It all went wrong.

ATTENDANT: Are you still sleeping?

FATIMA: I dozed a little. I dreamt of my brother who died young. They say if you dream of the dead and they want something from you, it's not a good sign.

ATTENDANT: So did he want something from you?

FATIMA: No. He just misses me.

ATTENDANT: Oh well, ready for your scrub? Turn over for me.

FATIMA: There was a house once right next to this hammam.

ATTENDANT: Where the car park is?

FATIMA: It was demolished after the war. It belonged to a decent family. Kind, religious people who helped me turn my life around. I lived with them and worked here in the hammam.

ATTENDANT: You said.

FATIMA: I did it so as to make an honest franc. We had francs then not dinars like now. The dinar came in 1964 after independence.

ATTENDANT: You have a good memory.

FATIMA: I memorise the Qur'an bit by bit. I practise every day.

ATTENDANT: Good for you.

FATIMA: *(to herself)* She wouldn't imagine, would she, the red life I lived? The men, the wine, the clothes, the looseness of it all. That gun that killed my brother, that same gun was one I had known so well…

FIFI: Raymond and I used to fool around with it in bed. The thrilling weight of it. I cleaned it one day. Then I put it in my mouth to make him laugh. Then I gripped it between my thighs.

FATIMA: I thought I had forgotten his face but I can see it clearly now.

24. Hammam (NOW)

Fatima is remembering a time from the past in Raymond's warehouse.

RAYMOND: *(distant, calling)* Hello?

FATIMA: The warehouse is full of boxes. He is counting them and he looks up. And I see his face.

RAYMOND: This is a surprise.

FATIMA: I remember the dress I was wearing.

FIFI: Black because I was still in mourning.

FIFI: The décolletée adjusted to be even lower.

FATIMA: Scent—

FIFI: Behind my ears, between my breasts—

FATIMA: Talcum powder—

FIFI: Under my arms.

FATIMA: But I was still sweating.

RAYMOND: How did you get in?

FIFI: You once showed me the side door.

RAYMOND: You have a good memory.

FIFI: And you said I would come back.

RAYMOND: Did I?

FIFI: I'm your *chienne*, remember?

RAYMOND: *(laughs)* You are.

FIFI: And you're my *maître*.

RAYMOND: I am. You're good, Fifi. You're good. You've come for more.

He touches her. Very close.

FIFI: I couldn't stay away.

RAYMOND: I told you.

They embrace.

FIFI: *(intimately)* And this.

RAYMOND: What?

FIFI: It's my brother's.

She stabs him as they embrace. He cries out.

FIFI: *(kissing him)* Shh. Shush, now.

She stabs him again, her hand over his mouth. He falls. She makes for the door.

FIFI: *(locking the door)* There's no one here.

Pause

What?!

REVOLUTIONARY: Your dress...

FIFI: You think a dress matters? Get on with it.

The Revolutionary walks around splashing petrol on the door. He stops.

REVOLUTIONARY: What was that sound?

FIFI: Nothing. Light the match. Hurry up.

The match is struck. The goods catch fire.

REVOLUTIONARY: They'll soon see that. Come on.

The fire starts to blaze.

REVOLUTIONARY: *(coming back)* What's the matter with you! Run, Fatima.

He grabs her and they run out. Fire sounds merge with that of the hammam's furnace.

25. The Hammam (NOW)

FATIMA: Straight away the weight of it. I wanted water.

FIFI: I came here.

The pouring of water

FATIMA: Every day, dark, always dark, and warm with the water all around me, scrubbing other women, cleaning their dead skin from the floor. Preparing a bride and acting all jolly. I had to carry coal for the furnace, I had to carry buckets of cold water, hour after hour, month after month.

ATTENDANT: There, nearly done. Stretch out your arm for me.

FATIMA: It's hard making an honest franc.

ATTENDANT: Are you back to the francs again?

FATIMA: Dinar.

ATTENDANT: Right. Other arm.

FATIMA: My brother bought me grilled corn with his first wage.

ATTENDANT: Corn on the cob?

FATIMA: Yes. It tasted so good. There was a blessing in it because it wasn't from tainted money. Do you get me?

ATTENDANT: Sure. (*Splashes her with water*) There you go.

FATIMA: I'm done.

ATTENDANT: Yes. All ready to dry up and get dressed again.

FATIMA: Thank you.

ATTENDANT: Remember me in your prayers, Granny.

Shazea Quraishi

Fallujah, Basrah

Fallujah, Basrah

A poem in four voices

i. Rahim
Oh my son

Let my love
cushion the weight of your head.

Let me take your hurt
    I will hold it

while you rest
I will fold it into my body.

Sleep, my angel,
my flower, my brave, sweet boy.

[Child with extreme hydrocephalus – deformity of face, body and ear – and defects of cerebral nerves.]

ii. Sabir
I dressed him in a long white shirt
with a blue bird embroidered over the heart
and placed tiny white mittens on his hands.
Born with thick black hair
like his father, he was almost
so beautiful, almost perfect
as we had imagined him.

[Born without eyes]

iii. Farrah
Where is my baby girl,
the one I dreamed?
I long for sleep
to return her.

[Extreme hydrocephalus. The line running down the right side of the head would appear to show that potentially two heads were forming.]

iv. Anah

[It isn't clear what has happened to this child.]

Cousin

You carry them on your back,
your muffled parents and her
soft, small children,
as you carry your sister's body
wrapped in its white shroud
over the bright, stony ground.

Now the brown earth pillows
her, holds her small body
in its quiet lap,
rocks her to sleep.

You may have heard of me

You may have heard of me
My father was a bear.
He carried me through forest, sky
and over frozen sea. At night
I lay along his back
wrapped in fur and heat
and while I slept, he ran,
never stopping to rest, never
letting me fall.
He showed me how to be careful as stone
sharp as thorn and quick
as weather. When he hunted alone
he'd leave me somewhere safe – high up a tree
or deep within a cave.
And then a day went on…
he didn't come.
I looked and looked for him.
The seasons changed and changed again.
Sleep became my friend. It even brought my father back.
The dark was like his fur,
the sea's breathing echoed his breathing.
I left home behind, an empty skin.
Alone, I walked taller, balanced better.
So I came to the gates of this city
– tall, black gates with teeth.
Here you find me, keeping my mouth small, hiding
pointed teeth and telling stories,
concealing their truth as I conceal
the thick black fur on my back.

The Mummy of Hor

In this cave-like room, lamp-lit,
the Goddess Isis spreads her wings
across Hor's chest to protect him.

But that's not all:
the four sons of Horus guard his entrails
and the human-headed God Imset guards the liver
while Ha'py, with a baboon head, guards the lungs.
Duamutef, who has a jackal's head, guards the stomach,
Quebehsenuf, with a hawk's head, guards the intestines
and other Gods watch over his body
while sacred symbols protect his soul.

Hor's body, wrapped in layers of linen
and bound with black pitch
is here
and you are gone.
    I think of you
    on that country road
    when your heart stopped
    and your breath stopped…

    I think of you there alone.

Gold

I crossed the land with my small
gold baby. I had only my skin
which hung from me in folds, to wrap him in,
only my hands to cover his miraculous feet.
We came to a forest where the trees had faces;

there was a loud ticking and the smell
of waiting – dry, leafy.
I thought of his soft heart, the blood like finest embroidery
running through his body, and I was heavy
with the knowledge of animals in the forest –

the claws and eyes, the beaky hunger.
My baby stirred and the trees leaned closer.
I walked till I came to a wall of grass
reaching over my head. Then I heard
a shushing that calmed me, though

it could have been wings beating or knives
slicing the air. The grass
parted, like a sea parting
and my baby's breath on my skin
was the wind in our sails.

Steps

Where I come from
we don't hang portraits of our beloved dead
to comfort us in empty rooms,
we hang their shoes, wrapped in gauze,
sewn with surgical thread.

In my hall I've hung
my father's shoes, their soft leather
shaped by his strong
brown feet shaped by his journey.
I close my eyes and see my father

walking towards me.
As the day closes, I press my ear
to the air around me,
listening for his footsteps,
his key in the door.

Note: In Fallujah, Basrah, *medical quotes come from Ross B. Mirkarimi of* The Arms Control Research Centre *in his May 1992 report* The Environmental and Human Health Impacts of the Gulf Region with Special Reference to Iraq, *commenting on photographs of extreme birth deformities experienced in Iraq and Afghanistan following bombing with DU incendiary devices. All names are fictional.*

The Mummy of Hor *uses text from museum labels for the* Mummy of Tem Hor *in Swansea Museum.*

Shaista Aziz

Blood and Broken Bodies

The bludgeoning to death of twenty-five-year-old pregnant Farzana Parveen, by members of her family for defying them and marrying a man of her choice, has once again put Pakistan at centre stage regarding the treatment of women.

It isn't just the mob outside the court in Lahore who picked up bricks and sticks to break Farzana's body that are responsible for her death. The blame also lies with a dominant toxic, patriarchal culture across large parts of Pakistan that deems women and girls as subhuman, property owned by men who can be discarded and tossed away in the blink of an eye and a 'justice' system that allows men to kill women with impunity.

Farzana Parveen is the latest name to add to a long list of women whose lives have been cut down in the land of the pure, Pakistan.

According to human rights and women's groups at least 900 so-called 'honour' killings have been carried out in Pakistan over the past twelve months. The term 'honour' killing is abhorrent and feeds into the narrative that killing a woman is justified. There is nothing honourable about killing a woman. There is nothing honourable about killing anyone.

A society is judged by the way it treats its most vulnerable. Pakistan's treatment of its most vulnerable, women, children and minorities, speaks volumes about the state of the nation. My beautiful motherland is sinking under a growing tide of blood and broken bodies. Each horrific killing leaves a lasting stain and a pain that throbs deeper with time refusing to fade.

I was seventeen when I first understood how little a woman's life is worth is in Pakistan. How the 'love' of a brother and a mother can lead to a woman, a girl, being hunted with brutality, killed and buried in an early grave.

I met Sania (not her real name) when I was sixteen and staying in my grandfather's village in Pakistan Kashmir. She had travelled to our village with her family from rural Punjab to visit some people. I remember Sania. She was sixteen. She was wearing a red scarf. She had beautiful almond-shaped eyes and whenever she was asked a question she would cover her mouth with the red scarf, look down and then whisper. Like most girls her age she was painfully shy.

Sania appeared curious to meet a Pakistani woman around her age from the West. Because of her shyness we communicated mostly through smiles and she spent a lot of time giggling at me.

The following year when I returned to the village and asked after everyone, I remembered Sania and asked how she was. My aunt raised her finger to her lips and told me to hush. She then pulled me inside the house and sat me down.

'She's dead. Her brother killed her. She was in the kitchen at the time. He entered the kitchen and told her that she was a shameful woman and had brought shame and disgrace on the family. He accused her of looking at a man. He then stabbed her over and over. We heard that she was stabbed at least twenty times.'

Sania's brother had killed her in the family home and nobody did a thing to stop him. The police had arrested him but he was released a few days later because their mother had forgiven him. A mother had forgiven her son for killing her beautiful daughter with the almond-shaped eyes. He was free to live his life while Sania was in the ground, covered by the soil of a country that continues to betray women like her.

A week into my trip I spotted Sania's brother, back in the village meeting friends. He was a tall man, he looked strong and arrogant. I observed him from the roof of our house as he swaggered past and felt a deep burning rage inside me.

Every time I returned to Pakistan I would hear countless stories through my female relatives and friends in rural and urban Pakistan of women being beaten – one was attacked by an axe and left for dead, another's body was discovered by her children when they returned home from school.

The newspapers were full of stories that tripped off the women's tongues almost like a weather report. Most of the time the women's killers were members of their own families and very rarely is anyone punished for their deaths.

Some of the strongest and bravest women I've met anywhere in the world are Pakistani. The housewives, teachers, students, health workers, doctors, human rights workers, lawyers, writers, journalists, activists and artists who step out of their homes not knowing if they will return in the evening. Many face the prospect of extreme violence in their own homes as much as they do outside them.

Qandeel Baloch, a twenty-six-year-old former model and social media star, became a household name in Pakistan for her bold, unapologetic videos celebrating her sexuality and, in turn, exposing the deeply ingrained misogyny and hypocrisy cutting across Pakistan's social and class divide.

She pouted, she purred, she provoked – oozing confidence rarely seen in most Pakistani women her age or any age – and uploaded videos on social media platforms for her hundreds and thousands of followers, the majority of whom were young Pakistani men.

They watched her videos behind closed doors with glee, and then hissed and cursed her publicly for her so-called 'un-Islamic and filthy ways.' In a country with reportedly one of the highest Google searches for pornography in the world, Ms Baloch became the target for the self-proclaimed male and female moral and religious police.

As one Pakistani man told me: 'She was like the forbidden fruit, tempting, eye candy that you knew was forbidden.'

In one of her most rebellious and political acts, Ms Baloch posed for selfies with an Islamic cleric. Perched next to the excitable figure while balancing his hat on her head and with a twinkle in her eye, she shook the cleric's hand and talked to the camera explaining she had borrowed his hat because she did not have a headscarf to cover her head.

In that one moment alone she took on Pakistan's religious lobby head-on by exposing hypocritical attitudes toward women. The video went viral and the backlash spread like wildfire; social media users in Pakistan called for Baloch to be taught a lesson or urged that Baloch should change her behaviour.

In July 2016, Ms. Baloch was drugged and strangled to death in the name of 'honour.' Her brother Waseem, twenty-five, now in police custody after going on the run, confessed to killing his sister because, he said, 'Girls are born to stay at home' and bring honour to the family. He went on to say he had no regrets over killing his sister and for him the video with the Islamic cleric was the final straw.

According to her brother, he killed her in the family home in Multan, Punjab, Pakistan's largest province, as their parents slept upstairs, proving once again that in Pakistan, as in other parts of the world, a woman is not even safe in her own home.

This is the same home from where Ms. Baloch says she was forced into an abusive marriage with an older man at the age of seventeen and, in her own words, endured years of 'torture' from her ex-husband. She gave birth to a son and then a few years later escaped to build her own life.

Ms. Baloch is the latest woman to be murdered by a family member in so-called 'honour killings' in Pakistan. Since May, there has been an increase in reported honour killings across Pakistan; women beaten and burnt to death. In one recent case a young woman's brother slashed her throat and watched her bleed to death. Her crime? She was accused of talking to a man on the phone.

The Human Rights Commission of Pakistan reports more than 1,000 women were killed for 'honour' in Pakistan in 2015. The prosecution for such crimes remains woefully low, with family members often forgiving the killers, who are also family members, so they walk free.

There has been a huge reaction to Ms. Baloch's murder in Pakistan and among the Pakistani diaspora around the world. Her death has opened a Pandora's box of misogyny even among Pakistani women and many other Muslim women, who are leading the hate charge by labelling Ms Baloch online and on social media as a 'prostitute', 'a filthy, dirty woman', a 'fornicator' and a non-Muslim.

The Islamic Republic of Pakistan continues to betray women like Qandeel Baloch, as do these so-called sisters drowning in hypocrisy and hate.

Miss L

Stand By Me

During the hype of the *Ghostbusters* remake, a memory came careering towards me. It was one of the memories that you see so small in the distance and, as it races up at you, curiosity is replaced by horror as you start to recognise what it actually is. Suddenly I'm ten years old, I'm with my friends and we're performing a full-length stage version of the film *Stand By Me* for our class. For about a week I laughed at the nerve of six ten-year-old girls thinking that this was a good idea, but once the laughter finally subsided, my disbelief at our sheer nerve took over. Every lunchtime, every day after school we were allowed to not go straight home, every morning we were all a little early, we practised this play. My friend Lucy and I were the instigators after having watched the film together with her two older brothers. For some reason, instead of running outside to play, we decided to script and direct our own version. Being ten, it didn't occur to us to ask boys to play the roles, of course not, we just decided that girls could play all the parts instead, and why not?

I look at the film industry now and I look at the film industry when I was growing up, and of course we put female characters at the centre of our performance. This story didn't exist where young girls could see themselves. TV and film told us that girls had to be pretty, with poker-straight blonde hair, long lithe limbs and an endless supply of pink and purple clothes. We didn't know anyone like that. We were girls who grew up in the countryside. We were brunette, chubby, wore cheap jeans and perpetually muddy trainers. We climbed trees, chucked dolls out of windows and made dens in the woods. Telly was telling us that we should be obsessing over boys and silver lipstick but all we were obsessing over was the fact that a partially obscured white plastic bag about 15 metres from our unscaleable school grounds fence was definitely hiding a dead body. So of course we watched this film of friendship and adventure and needed to put ourselves in it. No one was telling our story, they were telling the story of boys.

I wish I could go back and tell ten-year-old me that things have changed. That if she were growing up now there would be so many more things that she could relate to, things that wouldn't make her feel as if she was somehow doing it wrong because she had frizzy hair and a big nose and liked running around outside with muddy feet. I wish I could tell her that, when she grows up, there will be so many more things that tell her story. That, despite her first few experiences, she'll somehow have become an actress and that she'll be playing roles that reflect her reality. Her eyes will light up for a second when I tell her that *Ghostbusters* now has four women in it but I won't have the heart to tell her how much anger there was about it. And I'll never have the heart to tell her that no one that looks like her gets to be the hero. She already knows not being white makes things harder. She's been called 'Paki' in the street and I'm so proud that she was able to shout back and tell them that, if they're going to be racist, they should at least get it right. She doesn't know yet that, when a terror attack happens in 2001, she'll panic about her family and the fact that her and her dad are the only Arab-looking people in their little white village.

Before graduating as an actor, I'd played everything from Jack Frost to Gordie Lachance to a seventy-six-year-old woman, but, as I got older, the range of roles the world would let me play became narrower and narrower. By the time I was graduating from drama school, I'd been reduced to one role and one role only. Being a woman with an unpronounceable name and yellowy brown skin meant that I would only be allowed to play how the world saw me. My excitement at being an actress was quickly squashed by the realisation that all I was going up for was either terrorists of the wives of terrorists. Now, I'd been warned at drama school that this would happen but I never actually thought it would happen to me.

Very recently I finally had my first ever television audition. Television has always played a huge part of my life; both a comfort and a window to the world, it's a medium I've always held close to my heart. Given recent news events, I was unsurprised to see that I was up for the role of a refugee. She didn't speak but they claimed she was integral to the scene so I needed to audition for the role. Ten years of being an actress have taught me that I need to be grateful, even for the silent roles, so I went up like the obedient actress I am. A week or so later, I get a call from my agent telling me that, as the casting director loved me so much, he wanted to upgrade me to a speaking role. I remember hearing this while walking home and I could've cried in the street. Acting is so often about damning failure after damning failure but here I was, for once, being told that I was good enough. The girl who'd played Jack Frost was finally good enough. 'The only thing is, you'll be wearing a burka.' Smack. Five measly seconds I was allowed before being dragged back down to reality.

I felt I shouldn't be complaining because someone was willing to pay me to act. Despite all the hard work I've put in over the years and the fact that I actually deserve it, I'm still, of course, grateful for the work. I kept telling myself that the credit would be great on my CV. I tried cheering myself up by laughing at the sheer ridiculousness of it and the fact that this little tale completely summed up my acting career. But deep down I was gutted. Yet again I was being told that, as a Middle Eastern woman, no one gave a damn about what I'm able to represent. I can be anything. I proved that back in 1992 when I pretended to be a twelve-year-old boy who fainted when he saw a leech on his penis. Look at what that girl had done. This girl had done interpretive dance at the age of five in a tinsel wig and white tights to play Jack Frost. That girl was now being told that she was worth nothing more than a faceless figure uttering a couple of lines to further on the white man's storyline. Oh, and do you know what finally happened? Filming was delayed and they decided to do away with the scene. I'd cry if I wasn't laughing at the fact that nothing could sum up my acting career better.

So how do we change things? The problem is that yes, as Middle Eastern women, we have stories to tell. We owe it to other women to tell their stories, but we also have stories like everyone else's. Being a Middle Eastern woman doesn't mean you have to be in an arranged marriage or about to blow something up. Our real duty is to show young Middle Eastern girls that they matter just as much as that blonde-haired, blue-eyed girl in their class. They need to see themselves on screen, they deserve to see themselves on screen, and they deserve to pretend that there is a leech on their penis because they want to, not because they have to.

Aisha Mirza

Staying Alive Through Brexit

Racism, Mental Health and Emotional Labour

It's the night of the EU referendum. I am three thousand, four hundred and fifty-nine miles from London, my hometown, and I am scrolling. The UK is sleeping but New York is five hours behind and I am here, trying to pet the dog and have a nice time at a BBQ, while watching the votes get counted. I report the result of each area to my American friends like one of those text message services you didn't sign up for, and we talk about it even though none of us know what it means. I text my mum to tell her what has happened while she was sleeping and in the morning she replies, 'whatever happens, happens' which I momentarily mistake for apathy.

A few days later I am at New York PRIDE's Dyke March celebration. The music is good, the weather is good, I look good in the photos, my friends are nice and I am the most comfortably gay I have ever been. This should be a good or at least average day but I realise I am uncomfortable. My eyes are darting, focusing on everything and nothing and my chest is getting tighter with every step, until it almost feels solid. I recognise this as the beginning of a panic attack and excuse myself. As I leave, an intuitive friend asks me how I feel about Brexit. On a quiet corner I cry and gasp and try not to piss myself. Brexit. I have never felt so far from Home.

I am still awake at 5am, the tightness in my chest now a watermelon. It is hard to breathe. A dear friend from London has called and I struggle to speak loud enough for her to hear me. I am searching for hope like lost keys, it's here somewhere, I just had it. She tells me a story to try and cheer me up, a story in which all is not lost and London, in all its super-diverse glory, in all its tolerance, prospers. In this story, my friend witnesses a drunk English man in London tell a group of Eastern European women he does not know that he is so glad they are there. I tell her that is not a happy story.

And the unhappy stories keep coming.

'Haven't you gone home yet?'

'Paki.'

'Would you like a banana with that?'

I think about my mother as a child in Seventies Britain, quiet, skinny, hairy, brilliant. The oldest of four, she was tasked with protecting both her immigrant parents and her younger siblings from the constant threat of physical and psychic white violence. I think about my grandmother who kept a bucket of water underneath her letter-box just in case a burning rag or a firework visited in the night. I think about my sister, my cousins, their brown skin, their Muslim names. I try to stop thinking. Eventually I fall asleep with my fists clenched.

The leave voters are not the problem. They are the product of hundreds of years of colonial divide and rule, most recently implemented via a vicious austerity programme that has nothing to do with migration, and everything to do with keeping the elite rich. I am most fearful of the white middle class liberals who voted to stay, who think they are Good White People but are actually People With Power Who Never Listen Because They Don't Have To. These are the people who see themselves as separate from the leave voters *and* the black and brown people being attacked on the street; distinct, commentators with so much to say. I have spent hours, days and years in conversation with people like this, discussing structural inequality in the UK, isolation, fetishisation, why I had to escape – and still they seem to think racism started a week ago.

They are the people who really scare me, because after this recent spike of hate crime normalises, and we are left with the constant, low-key, micro-aggressive, soul-destroying racism that has always characterised life in the UK for people of colour, they will forget. They will continue to talk over us, to tell us we are 'moderate Muslims', to get paid to write and speak about things they know absolutely nothing about and to doubt us every time we try to talk about racism. To truly consider what life as a black or brown person of colour might feel like takes work – hard work, a rupture in a free existence and then inevitably, culpability. I have yet to meet a white person prepared to do that work, to step into that vulnerability. There are cheese and crackers that need to be eaten after all.

We can talk to the leave voters all we want, and we can blame old people if it makes us feel good, but they are not the people in charge now or in the future. They did not create this and this does not serve them. I am lucky enough to have experienced higher education among the elite, the artistic and political leaders of tomorrow. They are scary. They think their white liberalism is ***Flawless*. They pretend to listen but they do not hear a thing. They use our bodies and our stories, they hold us tight in photographs and they pretend they can't see us when we finally collapse, just like their daddies did. They put our heads on sticks and call it multiculturalism. They are the kind of people who will read this and think I am talking about someone else.

As the days continue, well-meaning Americans make conversation with me about Brexit. Every time, I feel a wave of sickness, pain in my chest and a scramble of thoughts, flashbacks, half-words, reveries. I hold my stomach and speak through long, measured breaths. Despite moving to New York on a scholarship to study the mental health effects of oppression, I am finding it so, so hard to admit to myself that a news story is making me feel as though I'm dying so many times a day. I wish the white people telling me that I need to be gentle, that I should talk to those who are different from me, had any idea what it feels like to be this tired.

We will talk. Right after we have dragged the UK's legacy of violence from under its ugly, expensive carpet, after we have learned it, taught it, remembered it, accepted it as an explanation for everything we see. We can talk after we have taught our children mental and physical self defense. We can talk after we have spoken to each other, about mental health, survival, and the anti-blackness we perpetuate within our own communities of colour, oppressing black people in a space they should be safe. We have lots to talk about. If only middle-class white people would stop talking.

In 1980 my mum, a first-generation Pakistani living in North London, won a writing competition aged sixteen, using the prompt An Event of Importance to my Community. In it she writes:

Today it is unsafe for any Asian person to walk down the street without his colour, speech, or dress being made fun of. You, the readers, may think that I am exaggerating, but the truth of the matter is, that noone has yet realised the seriousness of racial prejudice… I fear that by the time we grow up, we will be too full of bitterness simply to sit down and talk things over. If anything isn't done, we are going to explode and you will explode with us.

We explode every day and we piece ourselves together again. We explode for our ancestors, when we don't expect it, and then again when we remember. We explode every time our trust is abused, every time it becomes obvious noone heard us, every time we have to retreat, thicken our walls that keep us locked in, angry, safe. We explode.

Hibaq Osman

The Things I Would Tell You

The Things I Would Tell You

If you squint hard enough at our building
it starts to sink into the backdrop of
Green Dragon estate.
I've spent a lot of time sitting here squinting
turning pebbles into rhinestones,
this is the closest I will come.

Here,
clovers bet on each other
the first to lose its luck,
same way young boys kiss each other with bruises
they say 'this is how it'll feel when the world loves you.'
Seems you lost yours long before I knew what loss was
and between this place and the schools we shared
I find parts of you scattered.

I would tell you
I thought you were at The Pit,

lashes deep in the soles of every dream kicked into free goals,
every alleged mugging that went down
and weed pushed by policemen into the pockets
of men too young to inhale anything
but the pollution they were born into.

Immigrant kids speak a language
only broken souls can read,
same one you were fluent in.
You gave away a tongue and picked up another
padlocked language, recognised your lungs
in pages of Arabic script.

When your name is Amin
it's no wonder you found yourself
at the end of our prayers.

I would tell you
Mum has nightmares still
a fresh scar torn every day while I slowly forget your face
and if this world is a stage then brother I am nervous
shaking, pushing words out too fast,
trying to catch my breath
and tripping over things I haven't said yet.

I would tell you I am lonely,
the kind of lonely only ghosts of family members can fix –
the kind of lonely that just sits.
They say I am a woman now
but if this is womanhood they can take it all from me
there aren't enough clovers in the world
and your pictures are fading faster than I recall.

I've decided to stick to only counting your birthdays

it's one of the few things that keeps me from putting
and end to my own.

And now I'm here,
squinting at a building I don't live in any more
writing this for you
hoping it will be enough.

July and the Following Months

I think you are lucky
not because I feel you have not been through hardship
nor do I think everything has been handed to you.
I am sure you have worked to get to where you are
but I think you are lucky
not because I could walk a mile in your shoes
in fact, I am almost certain I could not take one step
out of my own body

but you are lucky
to be able to detach yourself from stories like this,
to enter and exit conversations as you wish
how you can drop your two cents and walk away –
you are lucky to be able to walk away.

How you can be called 'rational'
when you say things like 'at the very bottom of this case a man
was murdered, he should have been put away for that.'
While I wonder how it is so easy for you to call him a man
when I could only ever call him son, boy, child.
You do not have to carry this on your back.

On the night I found out about the verdict
I paced up and down my street, wondering who would
    be next
putting love hearts on post-it notes warning black families
not to watch the news the next morning.
Not guilty meant 'you are unworthy of our protection
    even in death.'
Not guilty was a white flag that did not mean surrender.
Not guilty told us even parents do not empathise
with the murder of our children,

that they will always be on trial
no matter who pulls the trigger.

You will always hold your right to bear prejudice close to heart,
you will distance our kids,
make them anything but human
just to see if you can still
hit the mark
from here.

I think you are lucky
to be able to have a bird's-eye view
while we stand in the middle of it,
one eye to the backs of us, the other on our feet
making sure we are ready when we need to
Run.

Matchstick Lips

You told me not to wear my words with a smile,
said this was not something I should want to caress in my
    palms,
not a crown I should wear
or a cheque I should cash.

We do not have the privilege of being asleep –
our bones ripped away from muscle,
sharpened and used as spears.
This is not a competition, not a talent,
only aching and oaths, only blood and scars.
This is no human song.

I'm not sure if I have ever been asked harder questions
than of the evening I told my mother I was a poet.
Says: daughter, are you proud of what you do?
She has many questions I do not have answers for.
Wonders if I am mourning,
if I've spilled enough tears to replace the ink
of all the pens I've broken out of frustration.

Says: daughter, this is not new to us,
this poetry born of so-called illiterate minds
of bloodshed and Moving and Moving,
do you not know you come from nomads?
There is no Home here or there
there is only journey,
there is only pebble-ground and bush fire,
there is only moonlight and struggle-hymn
this can't be a best seller,
an award winner,
this can only be truth.

Sharing yourself comes easy
when the stories you tell aren't your own.
You might pray for serenity
or the calm of closing lines
but I've learned
if you treat every poem like a eulogy
it's okay to feel like something in the room has just died.
Okay to profess your words as truths,
to speak from quivering lips and keep hands in pockets,
to never look the listeners in the eyes
for fear of losing yourself
for the final time.

Mother,
on the few occasions you've told me you loved me
you made it sound like an apology.
This is what I am running from
and also what I am running to.
I do not wear my words with a smile
and sadly
this is the only thing I have in common with you.

The One I Try to Forget

In the space between
clean clothes and fresh breeze,
I remembered all the times you apologised.
how I caught the drink off your tongue
Heavy scent on ripped shirt

Looking back, I do not think myself weak.
Survival is our every strained breath
and I have become accustomed to swallowing wind.

I'd ask you,
how dark was your hurt in daylight?
Have you rid yourself of a rotten heart? Rotten hands?
Did you pray for a sleep that did not come?
Have you ever, even once, touched a body with caution?

When you made your way back to
women who trust you
hiding my screams in your pockets
Where did the guilt go?

I store mine under my eyelids
I am reminded of you
If simply blink too hard.

A Year From Home

April
We were told the land had a whale's mouth
of ocean for each household,
free-flowing and unrestricted

I packed four necklaces that ward off evil,
Drooping eyelids, batteries
and bags of air in case I missed home

July
The school is called a 'comprehensive'
My cousins say this is a good thing,
the queen herself must know I am smart

August
There isn't as much water here as we thought
With bare feet I walk a patch of grass
the sun hell-ish ball of light
Burns insignia into my nape

November
I've shortened my words, y'know?
Sit at the sides of rooms and beg to be smaller,
My teachers don't look me in the eye

We don't have heavy tongues no more
I whisper my words into nooks and crannies
This is how the English are

February
Worship here is different too,
There's no spirit to feel,

Only eyes at the back of my head

My great-aunt taught me how to sigh
She'd say: soft but deep, soft but deep
Or the ancestors won't hear you

In this land, they are all you have.

Azra Tabassum

Brown Girl

Brown Girl

(After Megan Falley)

Brown girl,
be quiet, quieter,
softer. Dumb
yourself down, read less,
don't think so much
about the knots in your belly.
How it hurts when they
tell you brown girl
don't laugh too loud,
don't say too much.
Brown boys don't want it,
don't like it.
All your dance, all your giggle.
Your spine or your knuckles,
those boldfaced ugly opinions.
How dare you, brown girl,

put your chin up, meet their gaze
head on?
Where is your shame?
Who will want to marry you,
with that attitude?
With that snake tongue?
With all your fire and your venom.
Brown girl keep your eyes down,
brown girl keep your legs shut,
brown girl, disappear,
slowly, gently,
so they don't see you dimming.
Turn in on yourself.
Switch the lights off.
Brown girl, listen.
When your auntie tells you
sshhhhhh,
when your mama says
your hips are too big,
your mouth is too wide,
and those words, the bite of them,
how could you, brown girl,
be more than that, how could you?

Green Street

She was there like that,
in the gauze of Green Street,
wrapped in an emerald sari,
her mother's, her grandmother's,
centuries tucked in creased
crêpe linen at her waist.

Eyes on the brown boys,
cast downwards. Up again.

A man offers her cheap eyeliner.
£1.50.
Only a pound if it comes
with a smile.

He swarms in her direction
like a wasp, buzzing
for the sweat of her skin.

'Not today.' She tells him.

Somewhere on Green Street,
someone is sinking their teeth
into a hot chicken samosa,
wincing.

Pernicium

The burning houses came first –
and then the people.

Growing new limbs from strange places.

Hands sprouting from necks,
wanting – to be touched again

   and not touched, again,
there was silence and then   nothing

once, long ago   faceless children
   pressed fingers into fingers

rolled in the sandpits together –
before regret,

loose-limbed and uncanny
grew like ivy around them

and turned them sallow, milk-less,
   crumbling in the wind

   from the ceilings and the sky,
un-filling the bodies, again

– the mothers who lost their babies
and ran howling into the wind after them,

   how they came back empty-handed
with new eyes in their foreheads
clutching handfuls and handfuls

And God, And God

The dead crawl out of the woodwork
soft hands, soft thighs, dripping eyes and wombs,
mouths first and swollen with words.

The women.

My grandmother leads the procession.
She meets me in my bedroom
against that fading light

To tell me she is sorry that love
was an untangle of veins inside of her,
how he is still cradled against her hips

Even now, the callous of his hands,
hard against her caramel brittle bones
sharing all that unshed warmth.

The men.

My uncles, not the bedroom – it is too intimate,
the kitchen, where they talk about tiling,
and ask me why my hair is so short

To tell me that God is as gentle
as we'd thought, and taller
than we could ever believe.

My father.

He comes with his heart softening
in his hands like melted butter,

the question mark of his mouth turned inwards

To ask me how I could spill lies so easily
from the same throat we shared, half and half,
him and my mother and the man.

My mother, but the man I love.
My father, but the man I love.
And God and God
and God.

Selma Dabbagh

Take Me There

He'd walked by her when he got back. It was late, which had meant she'd had to sleep in the afternoon before he returned if she was going to keep herself awake until he returned. But even when you took average times into account, he was late. He did not speak as he came in, but placed his collection of laminated IDs and paper permits on the table next to the front door, pushing them under the tissue box, so that they were far enough away as to not be seen, but not too far from reach, in case the soldiers came that night. He remembered to do this, but he neither hung his jacket on the hook, nor removed his shoes. They muddied the corridor with packed sand as he passed her, neither taking in her ironed shirt, nor the way she had arranged her hair, which was in a style she had not tried before.

He could not avoid the food though, there were ways she had been taught to bring a good man like him around and to keep him to heel and this was one of them; the vine leaves were smaller than a baby's finger and she knew they were better than his mother's. Abu Rasha had supplied the wine, three bottles at a decent price and these had been lain on their side on a rack he had constructed out of bamboo, nails and pipe cleaners following instructions he had found on YouTube. He did not talk during the meal. He looked up once and raised his eyebrows, at the shirt, the rearranged hair and let them fall again to the plate as though he was saying, If you expect action, you'll be needing another man. He found no fault with the food and told her one benign event from the day, one little insight into gossip from the man in front of him at the turnstile who was a cousin of a woman she had been at school with. It was neutral information about a work permit being obtained and she had learnt not to seize upon this kind of disclosure as though she needed it, or to feign excessive interest, in a way that could come across as being patronising, by trying to make the day seem better than it was. Behind him, above the sink, the curtains were drawn to keep out the concrete that took everything away from them, and to block out the glare of the spotlights that were affixed to the top of it. They preferred it that way, but at one point he turned around to check on it as though wondering what was wrong.

She watched his hands during the meal. He was half qualified as a vet and you could tell that by the way he ate, particularly with the lamb, a careful removal of fat, a separation of tendon from muscle, the occasional curious manipulation to check on the mechanics of the joints. The unqualified half of him, which had abridged the first, was manual worker, an outdoor profession that boiled a sore blush into his cheeks and branded a dark tan down from the line where the T-shirt ended. After the food and the one glass of wine, he asked her what had happened in the other place she sometimes spoke of,

'Tell me about it,' he had said, his eyelashes, despite his wash, still slightly crusted by the sweat of the day, 'take me there.'

'There was a young guard,' she started, wanting to make it new, but not too unchartered to be clumsy. She could lose him with one erroneous detail, 'on the Eastern side, he had an allergy to a flower, a little similar to the yellow flower that grew on the land of the Hamza family at the base of their hills.' She'd messed up already, by making references that were too close to them, to problems that surrounded them,

'I know the one,' he said, letting her off, and she continued,

'He'd always been short for his age until he was thirteen when he shot up and became tall like a reed, but he was too attached to his mother, hating the porridge she made him every morning, but loving everything else about her.'

'Why should I know about the soldiers on that side?' He said, 'On the East, why should I care for them?'

'Because without recognising their humanity we have no chance that they will recognise ours.'

'You don't know what they're like,' he snapped now; his look was like a kick, a reproach that she refused to be cowered by, 'This morning, the sons of bitches—' he swore again, 'those—'

'He didn't want to be posted to the watchtowers, but he had no choice and he came when already many who tried to cross from East to West had been shot. One morning he saw a girl, about the same age as his cousin from Leipzig, with a similar long, dark plait, run until she was mown down. She lay in no man's land fallen over one arm, crumpled, as the boy she was with turned back once then tried to run zigzagging to the other side before he was shot too and—

'Tell me how they got rid of it. I need to hear about that. Tell me that.'

'People from across the whole city, old men and women, boys, girls, they all came to take it down. Their wall was sprayed with graffiti, it was not as tall as ours, but it was strong, made of cement as well, it was there so long that no one believed it would go. They grew up under it, families were separated by it, people died trying to cross it and yet they came the people of that city, they came and broke at it with sledgehammers and pickaxes and anything they could find.'

'I know how to use a pickaxe.' He grazed the callouses on his palm over across her cheek. But she was seeing it herself now. 'It was the people first, before they brought in the heavy equipment, the cranes and diggers that dismantled it more methodically.'

She walked behind him and pulled back the curtain that hid the wall. It started one metre from their house, rose eight metres into the sky and ran on for ever. Nothing weathered the wall; it stood pristine. It was free of graffiti at this point, for here it had been constructed in a private garden and they had managed to keep the local boys out. They did not want to be screamed at with messages that they already knew.

'Look,' she continued at the view which gave them nothing to see. 'When they take it down, we will see beyond to our land, which they will have to give us compensation for, for the time that we have not been able to benefit from it, for the way it has stopped you being able to continue your studies.'

'Compensation,' he mocked.

'It may take a while, we will have to be patient, they will need to set up bodies, requiring administrators, specialist knowledge will be sought internationally.' He was behind her now, sweetly acid with wine, languorous with fatigue; he leant on to her so that she was pushed up against the kitchen cabinet, bent forward.

'Show me what we'll see when it is gone.'

'We must remember that we lost three lemon trees and two mature apricot trees, we can record that on the claim form. The land will be bare and messy for some time, but it will recover, once you are back with it, it will feel the difference. You won't have much time because your practice will be very successful, but I will help, our children will too—' He had turned her around now and pushed her back so that she was seated on the work surface of the kitchen. He separated her legs so that he could lean between them, before he brought her forward again.

'And we will see the Hamzas' hills in the distance?'

'We will see again the Hamzas' land in the distance and the mountains of Jerusalem behind.'

The next morning he woke before she was able to get up to make the coffee. 'Don't get up for me,' he said, tracing along the line of her earlobe, 'but take me back won't you, tonight?'

'Berlin?'

'Berlin.'

By the time she woke up, he had cleared the plates, brushed away the sand from the hallway and put the tissue box that he hid his ID and permits under, back in its place.

Selma Dabbagh

Last Assignment to Jenin

If asked when I knew the direction events were going to take, I would say I never knew. I say that to myself now. There are some directions that are not imaginable.

He said our lives may be entirely restricted, but our imaginations are free. He said free as stars. He believed orbits were necessary for freedom. Without orbits, choice would be oppressive. 'You can't just spin,' I'd said.

Watch me! he'd replied, his face circling mine, up close.

Imagination is not limitless. It mainly takes us to good, safe places. I did not anticipate his departure, or his loss. Even at the point when he grabbed my arm and the undercarriage was upon us, there was disbelief.

Or hope, if you prefer.

Once I reached the edges of the camp, the realisation as to quite how screwed up everything was had come to me in an inarticulate, visceral way. It had started pounding through me. Once there, it had become clear that I could go no further.

I'd called him from an alleyway and, by doing so, I had pulled him into the mess I'd thrown myself into. Before my call, he'd been safe and he could have stayed that way. The alleyway was a dead-end about a metre wide with iron doors on either side which were bolted from the inside at three different heights. I had tried everything with those doors, but the inanimate inhabitants behind them stayed mute. If they had responded, I would not have called him.

I knew he was in the area. I had ways of always knowing where he was. In the seven and a half weeks before that evening, I'd started to dial his number more times than I care to admit to. But in that alleyway, I'd gone through with it.

I'd called him. He'd answered. We spoke.

After I called, the sense of having fucked up my life and now being about to do the same to his, swelled so huge in me that I felt that it, that feeling of fuckedupness alone, would burst down the sides of the alleyway: the feeling, not the enemy, you understand; a logical way to think when the enemy has, for so long, been the feeling.

It was a recent development to be able to see the hills from where I stood. The buildings opposite were freshly demolished providing me with an alley-framed vista of the rocks that were absorbing the sun. A chiffony veil of dusk caught on the hills and everything about the view said: For This. For this land we fight and die for ever.

It flaunted its bluey-green earth, its pinky-orange sky, and the line between the two swam as the crushed colours spread between each other. Here, said the land, presenting me with yet another scandalously beautiful evening about to fall dark.

It is transience that gives rise to beauty, not the object itself. The ownership of the thing is irrelevant. This, at least, was what I had been trying to persuade myself in recent months. But even a thought like that made me want him, for he placed views into context, turned ideas into philosophies.

I wanted him. I wanted him. I wanted him always. It spiralled in my head like a snail shell of childish handwriting: I want you back, now. Come back to me and so on. It was tedious and below me but it insisted on crawling into my ear whenever I was still, so I kept myself busy. This is what my friends told me to do when they were tired of me calling late at night.

It is common, I understand, when dumped, to dwell on your possible errors and personal flaws. I tried to accept this, but it was hard. I was bombarded by self-mockery: while driving, working, conducting a conversation. Waiting to pass through the turnstile at the Qalandia checkpoint, I'd once, at the memory of involuntarily passing wind during the sexual act, found myself hitting at my forehead in shame.

'*Maalik*? What's wrong with you?' the women queuing in front of me had asked, 'Aren't you used to the wait?' Although this self-abuse was a perpetual torment, it was nothing compared to the thoughts of how good it had been. The memory of his arm behind my waist pulling me down onto him - that alone could floor me for what felt like weeks. I started to shrivel as though drawn inwardly, my skin pulled tight over awkward bones. The mere sight of the words 'Kiss me!' scrawled over a wall's political graffiti could cause me to spend an afternoon behind my bed with my nails embedded into to my scalp.

I have no memory of eating during that period. I do recall picking the skin off some soaked chickpeas that my mother had left out in preparation for some maftool, but I don't remember actually consuming them.

Why the hell was it that I was in Jenin on that day, at that time? I would ask that too. I could answer that it was my job to go to places like that. This is the answer if I want to portray that the forces were greater than me, but it would not be an honest response. The truthful answer is that I had wanted the situation, its desperation; its extremity.

I understood it. It spoke to me.

That Jenin attack was the first of its kind, the worst of its kind. Its viciousness was stunning, even to us. Now such events are more common, but, at the time, that onslaught conveyed such a hurt that I felt I was alone in being capable of comprehending it.

Yes, yes, it was all about him. I thought that horror, diving into that external horror could turn off my own internal one.

On the phone I'd given him directions: I'm across the road from where the small mosque and the garage with the green tiles were, I had said.

– Were? He had asked.

– Were. I had confirmed. Then my battery had gone.

I called him. He answered. We spoke and then I stood. I even smoked. This was unorthodox for me. Hatem, the other fieldworker had left his cigarettes in my bag. I'm not a standing-in-an-alleyway kind of a smoker, it should be understood. I sit when I smoke, with coffee or a glass of wine and I always make sure that the ashtray is clean before I light up.

I had hoped smoking might distract me from the tanks and bulldozers moaning and slipping in the valley below, but I could think only of drones and night vision as I made a little orange star in front of my face with the cigarette of the fieldworker who got away.

I could not have stayed in the last witnesses' house. I'd made my excuses (lies) about people and transport and had left, by which time the streets were empty and the only cars remaining in the streets were those that had already been shelled.

That level of fear is like being in a pressurised container – it's the only way to describe it: a vacuum is created that winds you huh! until the lid is released, balance is restored, you are able to breathe again and then baf! you are winded once more. What I had not expected though was the sense of elation that runs alongside the fear, in a prattling endorphin-bolstered rush. Perhaps it is to do with oxygen manipulation.

The bulldozers and tanks comforted each other in the valley below – we're going up there soon, but we shouldn't worry, there are so many of us and we're together, with all the world behind us.

And ahead of them, behind me, were bodies, in the corners of rooms curled over themselves in front of televisions. Soft, waiting bodies in collapsible concrete cubes.

Maybe we had a lone gunman, possibly two. Okay, a handful. Some guys who knew how to booby-trap tiles. A couple of fellows who were dab hands with incendiary devices.

A God.

Ours against yours, okay?

On the phone he said – you know they are planning to attack again tonight?

As though I didn't know anything.

But I'd had to leave that last house. I couldn't stay there, not with all those ghosts. They were sucking up all the air. '*An jad* you've got to take me seriously with this one. The little buggers had been seeking me out for weeks. At home, they would come tiptoeing across the stone floor in the half-light of morning. When the first girl came, I'd thought she might be bringing me messages from him. But that was not their purpose. They were polite children who used speech with care, 'Look Auntie,' that first ghost girl had said, twirling in the greyish air, pointing at the part of her head that was no longer there, 'Look Auntie, half of it has gone. The soldiers blew it away.'

The ghosts had been more enthusiastic than normal in that last house: pulling at my trousers, willing me to talk to them, peering up at me from under my questionnaire. They chattered irrepressibly: a band of translucent, despairing monkeys on speed.

A fieldworker is essentially a form-filler in a flak jacket. My organisation doesn't support the wearing of flak jackets although our funders argue that we should sport this protective attire. My organisation's position is that the wearing of military-style outfits places a distance between us and the witnesses that we interview. I subscribe to my organisation's position and I do not wear a flak jacket.

Everyone said that I was good at my job. I was thorough and conscientious. Where my skills were lacking was in putting myself (and therefore also my witnesses) at ease. I admit I was a little hung up about being a 'middle-class' Jerusalemite. My bare head was also offensive to many of the families I visited, (on principle I would never cover it up). As a result of these 'barriers to communication', as the workshop trainers put it, I frequently adopted an imperious front with my witnesses: I expected them to serve me coffee, to turn on their fans, to offer me their best chair, not to interrupt my questions, or challenge my worth. At the same time, I felt humbled and useless in their presence. I was frequently possessed by the thought that they knew the details of my failed sexual relationships and that they therefore understood why I was an unmarried, childless woman in my mid-thirties. To stop them pitying me, I bossed them around. It was better, at least, to be hated.

At the last witnesses' house I had barked out question six without even thinking – 'Were the children warned before they were shot?' I'd asked Umm Hassan who had seen the whole incident from the downstairs window. The question had the effect of making the family look towards the door, as though an oddly dressed stranger had just walked in.

One of Umm Hassan's sons stepped in to disperse the white noise that my question had created, 'As my mother explained to you over the telephone, the soldiers were telling the children to pull down the wall that had been damaged, to move the bricks, and the children were crying because they were scared of the guns that were being pointed at them.'

'I see,' I said, scribbling at my form although the information didn't fit the box. Had a little ghost girl not been at my feet showing me her scratched and bloody palms, I may well have started winding up the interview then. There was a terrible smell of death in that room. If you don't know what death smells like, I can explain. It's like lumps of rancid, urban snot in your nostrils. It is not the kind of thing that can be dislodged by a tissue or a change of scene. Once you've smelt it, it will always be with you. It may abate before it recurs, but it's always there. It could come back to you in the most expensive restaurant in Geneva. Umm Hassan's family had been trying to counter it with bleach, air fresheners and disinfectant. The toxically cleansed surfaces of the room were still wet, the air was trying to pass itself off as Lily of the Valley, but all we could smell was death.

'They were trying to pick up the bricks and carry them, but the children were small and they were panting... they couldn't get enough breath...'

'Huh, huh, huh,' said Umm Hassan, her shoulders moving up and down, her chest contracting like a dog sweating on its side in the sun.

'Yes,' the son continued, 'they were breathing like that and the soldiers were aiming their guns at them, watching them run up and down, carrying the bricks and stones... telling them that they would be shot if they did not do it. But–'

Umm Hassan was staring at a spot on the wall above the chipped veneer sideboard with a gilt-decorated tray on it. Her son watched her revisit a scene that was being recalled and replayed for my benefit.

'But they shot them anyway,' she concluded with a shrug.

'Will the UN give us an extra bag of sugar if our answers are sufficiently precise?' asked Umm Hassan's son.

'It's not exactly for the United Nations, but we are hoping to document evidence of war crimes...' I had started and that was enough. Oh, the seduction of that term! After that, I couldn't stop them. The names of the children overwhelmed me. I was writing in a pad by now, exasperated by the form's lack of ambition, who was whose brother, which girl it was in the red skirt trying to help her three-year-old sister in the blue. There was no stopping it and I scribbled and scratched until way past the hour I had set as the absolutely latest time to leave, while the ghost children, orderly now, stepped up and presented themselves as though I was their teacher, or (God forbid!) their only mother.

He came. He was coming! He had come to get me out of there. The sound of a car travelling far too fast over a bumpy surface, the screeching of tyres audible over drones, helicopters and tanks – that was the sound of him coming for me to get me out of there.

He came! He came! He came!

'Who left you here?' he shouted, chucking stuff (a child's drawing, a first aid kit, a camera lens) off the passenger seat.

'Hatem. His wife was in labour.'

'He should never have left you here. Never.' He was holding the steering wheel in a melodramatically fierce way. I could see the slubs in a blue vein that ran on either side of his middle knuckle. It was him. In the shirt he had worn that evening in Ramallah when he had twiddled the gardenia stalk in his fingers round and round until I pulled it from him and stuck it in his hair for he was too shy to place it in mine. 'But you're okay?' he asked, 'You look okay.' Quiet. It was quiet, that last line.

'I'm fine,' I insisted, 'I just messed up my exit strategy, that's all.'

'You certainly did that.' He was looking upwards through a dirt smeared windscreen as he said this because it was clear that one of the helicopters was taking the same path as us. He accelerated, launching us against the rubble-strewn roads, grating at them with the bare-piped stomach of his Fiat.

'That way,' I said, although, in truth, I didn't really know. In darkness, the town had transformed itself again. It was more whole now, more resolute. The human diggers had gone: the men, women and children who had clawed at rubble with spades and hands. Either side of us were tombs of brick, wire and mattresses. The remaining houses were expressionless in the dark. Shuttered up and shut up, sprayed and scrawled with army graffiti that they didn't agree with.

He was trying to drive fast but the roads weren't allowing him to. We kept hitting things and being thrown by them.

'I heard you were in the area. I–' Even then, I was not considering what it was that was about to happen to us.

'We may be safer on foot,' he said, but he did not brake or give me a chance to get out. Tank engines could be heard, even above the strains and skids of the car, the hell of the helicopter. I still had to know, more than anything, I had to know, 'What happened to her?'

'To who?' He shouted, loud, angry like a father. The helicopter was hovering right over us, thwacking away as though the sky were made of tyre rubber.

'The bride your mother found to replace your unsuitable girlfriend,' I was screaming. His face turned up to the hovering weapon. A slam of brakes.

'Get out!' he screamed, 'Get out!'

'Okay, okay–' I leant forward to get my bag (my bag!?) pulling at the door with the other hand.

He grabbed my arm, made me face him, look at him. His eyes hard, steady, but talking, talking, like I see them now.

'She was a mistake, okay? The whole thing. She was a big mistake. Now get out. Get out–'

It was at that point that the shelling began.

Asma Elbadawi

Belongings

Belongings

Before I am stripped of my belongings
no tangible hold on the memories I harvested,
there is much to do.
I will one day have to answer to a man that is not my father
and he may not be as understanding.
This man wasn't there on the first day of nursery,
me standing at lanky school gates in my pink
    summer dungarees.
This man wasn't there the day I confessed maths is my weakness
and though I admire the accurate craft of an architect
my hands were not created to build soaring skyscrapers
    and houses:
I am changing my degree.

This man wasn't there to summon me for breakfast, lunch
    and dinner
(everyone knows I cannot cook
I spent my childhood playing cricket, rounders, netball, pool).

He wasn't there to know that the only sibling I have is a brother
so I know more about toy hot wheel cars and BB guns
than I do of Barbie and Ken.

This man wasn't there all the times I fell and grazed my knee
all the times I couldn't stop crying
all the times I couldn't stop laughing
all the times that I embraced my stretching zone
time and time again I question
is it time to give it all up
before it's officially time to pick up and uproot?

This man may never understand
that my whole life I worked towards the women I am today.
The clothes I give away
have remnants of my life sewed in them
the watches I wore
tick between chapters of my adolescence
the bags I carried
held me from one country to another.
The name I give away is the name that was used to register me
every day at school
on my passport and birth certificate.

How is it that we erase the history of a women
as if nothing mattered before her wedding day?

Summer

Winter came
and like every one before it I longed for summer.
I have been here for decades,
you would think my flesh would have tightened
to accommodate the short days,
thickened to fight the pinching cold,
the pearl white crumbling snow.
But after that last leaf falls every autumn,
I long for summer again.
The 6 weeks between school years,
between two entities
two me's infused with relatives and screaming kids.
Relatives I didn't know existed
until I was in between 11 and 12
and I gazed up at him.
My small body reaches half way between the top of his head
and the sandy ground beneath his shib shib.
I confidently call out in to the thick night 'Baba'.
I feel the burning of my cheeks as I realise he is not my father
Mother interrupts my embarrassment with her familiar laugh
Da amic Maki ya Asma, akho abook
This is your uncle Maki, Asma, your daddy's brother.
I have never heard the term brother used in this way.
Brother was Mohammed.
The idea that family was bigger than what I could see
hits the almost 12-year-old me with a tidal wave of
        awkward heat.

I guess winter only ever comes to remind me of the warmth
        of summer,
parts that are missing but always adorned.
Summer lives in the cracks of my skin,

the smile of my grandfather,
the cries of a new-born cousin
and the laughter of the Nile.

Samira Shackle

My Other Half

You ask me about that country whose details now escape me.
I don't remember its geography, nothing of its history.
And should I visit it in memory,
It would be as I would a past lover,
After years, for a night, no longer restless with passion,
With no fear of regret.
I have reached that age when one visits the heart merely
   as a courtesy.

Faiz Ahmed Faiz

We were the only women on the plane, my mum and I. The London-Dubai leg of the journey had contained a more mixed demographic, but the final stretch, Dubai-Karachi, pretty much entirely consisted of migrant labourers, taking a break from their work in the Gulf to go home for the holidays.

'This plane is full of peasants,' Mum whispered to me, loudly. She was a self-avowed feminist and socialist, but this proud egalitarianism went completely out of the window when it concerned her Pakistani compatriots. I assumed it was a hangover from the intensely class-bound society in which she grew up.

She hadn't really wanted to go; the trip was my doing. My mother was born in Karachi in 1950, three years after this new nation was born out of Partition from India in 1947. She moved to London with her parents and three siblings in the 1970s, when she was in her twenties. Her last trip back had been in the early 1990s, when my brother and I were small. She's a proud Pakistani who rarely wears western clothes and doles out Urdu proverbs at every opportunity. Yet, she said, she simply hadn't felt the need to return. Her immediate family is scattered over the globe; parents and brother in the UK, sisters in India and Bangladesh. London became the centre of gravity for our geographically dispersed family, the central point where everyone converged to enjoy and endure each other's company throughout the summer months, a cacophony of loud voices and strong personalities that grew together despite the vast distances between us in our daily lives.

The trip to Karachi, then, was because of me. It was 2011 – twenty years since our last visit to Pakistan – and, I'd decided, time for me to understand more about this society, at once so familiar and so mirage-like. Growing up in a multicultural area of London, I'd never given a huge amount of thought to my mixed heritage. I was English and I was Pakistani; a Londoner with an exciting first name and ambiguous colouring. I didn't speak Urdu and wasn't religious, but could recite Islamic prayers if necessary and utter the most basic Urdu phrases: hello, goodbye, how are you. I could cook Pakistani food and knew how to greet my elders respectfully. The culture – folklore, family history, geography – was soaked into the background of my life. My mother is a mythology fanatic, and my father, although English, is an academic who specialises in the languages and religions of South Asia. This country was so often misrepresented to the world, reduced to a collection of crude stereotypes: corner shops, jalfrezi, terrorism. As an adult, working as a journalist, my interest in my mother's homeland grew. I had never visited this country – at least, not while I was old enough to remember – but I felt that I instinctively understood it, a generationally transmitted knowledge from my grandparents, my mother, my aunts and uncles. It was mine.

A few months before we boarded that plane, I'd curated a special issue of the *New Statesman* (where I worked as a staff writer) on Pakistan. I had drawn on my network of family friends for what I'd planned to be a rich and different take on the country. It didn't look only at Kashmir and militancy, but also at the country's rich literary history and flourishing arts scene. The issue was a success and I'd had lots of congratulations on the contents, but, due to factors outside my control, it had been published with a picture of a giant cartoon bomb on the cover. To avoid any chance of misunderstanding, the bomb was painted with a Pakistan flag. It hardly did anything to dispel stereotypes, which had been my overwhelming aim in putting the package together. I was mortified. Blinded by maternal love, my grandmother still determinedly distributed the magazine to her extensive network of Pakistani expatriate friends, who politely congratulated me on the contents without mentioning the cover. I wondered whether they were just used to it.

Editors were quite happy to take my ethnic origins as evidence of my authority to write on Pakistan, but I began to feel I should go there and see for myself if I actually understood as much as I thought I did. After all, what does it really mean to be 'from' somewhere, if you've spent your entire life thousands of miles away?

Persuading Mum wasn't the easiest task. 'I don't like the heat,' she said. 'I don't like long flights. Actually, I don't really like Pakistan.' But, eventually, the calls were made to her cousin Sumayra in Karachi – my aunt, in the south Asian way of describing family relations. One of the many anomalies of my family was that my mother and her siblings had never held Pakistani passports; their grandfather – my great-grandfather – had been a Knight Commander of the British Empire, so the family had been given British passports at birth. Accordingly they never really considered themselves immigrants when they moved to the UK, despite the fact they had grown up in Pakistan. I'd never had any Pakistani identification either, so Mum and I both applied for visas, and the flights were booked. There we were, on a plane, heading towards a homecoming of sorts.

A heavy-set man pushed past me to get his luggage out of the overhead carriage. Grumpy and tired after eight hours of travel, I shot him a filthy look and sighed ostentatiously. Mum grabbed my arm, with panic in her eyes. 'You mustn't fight with these villagey types,' she said, horrified, after he'd sat down. 'You don't know how they'll react to an assertive woman.'

I decided it wasn't the time to discuss her inconsistent class politics. And anyway, the flight from Dubai to Karachi, a coastal mega-city in Pakistan's south-west, was mercifully short, which meant limited opportunity for Mum to offend anyone. I settled back into my seat and closed my eyes.

As the plane landed an hour later, clapping and cheers broke out. The man in the seat in front of us leant forward, his hands clasped. '*Alhamdulillah apni sar-zameen peh pohonche*,' he said, his voice full of emotion.

Mum translated for me. 'He said "Praise God, we have arrived on our earth, under our sky". It means we've come home, to the land that we belong to.' I looked at her. She had tears in her eyes.

◆

Karachi, city of lights, home to more than 20 million people, doesn't exactly have a good reputation. Mum and her siblings had always spoken about it as a cosmopolitan, coastal paradise, a swinging city that had been the proud capital of Pakistan upon Partition in 1947, the jewel in the crown of this new country full of promise. Even before my family left in the 1970s, government had migrated to the new capital, Islamabad, a planned city located closer to the middle of this enormous country. Since then, the security situation in the country at large had deteriorated, along with governance. And Karachi had become known primarily for crime, terrorism, and political violence.

Before leaving, I made the mistake of looking at the Foreign Office's travel guidance, which at the time could pretty much be summarised as 'don't go'. (This was 2011 and there had been an upsurge in political violence, with murder rates skyrocketing). The threats were constantly referenced by friends and relatives – practically everyone seemed to have a story about being held at gunpoint or kidnapped – but whiling away afternoons in palatial houses, eating an array of delicious fried snacks, it didn't feel particularly immediate.

There was a constant, dizzying stream of relatives I'd never met before, some I'd never even heard of. Cousins, aunts, uncles, great-aunts, great-uncles, friends of my grandparents, friends of my mother's, friends of my aunts'. 'Look! It's Samira, Shahrukh's daughter, Ahmed Husain's granddaughter. Aren't you tall? Aren't you fair? Didn't you go to Oxford?' But after these initial exclamations, what surprised me most was the fact that I wasn't much of a novelty at all, despite my fair skin and English accent. As soon as I'd been placed within the family web, understood as part of the network of Karachi society, I was immediately accepted, unquestioningly enveloped into this huge tapestry of people I had never known.

◆

It was March and the weather was starting to heat up, although there was a delicious sea breeze that managed to cut through the sharp, dry heat, even on the warmest days. I sat in the garden next to the pool, surrounded by sumptuous greenery, delicate yellow and white frangipani flowers, and vibrant bursts of red and orange hanging from the trees above. I wanted to wear my bikini so I could get a tan, so my aunt Sumayra told the servants (there was a small army of them) not to come outside. This was ostensibly to stop them from leering, but I suspected it was also to prevent their minds from being corrupted by the sight of a practically naked woman blithely wandering around, in a place where it's highly unusual to show your knees in public.

Sweat dripped off my forehead onto the page of my book; the air was baking hot, but I didn't want to admit defeat. I was sitting outside in defiance of a series of woeful, direly serious warnings from relatives about the risk to my health. An older relative looked distressed when I mentioned my plans to bronze my skin. 'You've been blessed with a fair complexion, and this is what you do?' Someone else warned me that I could expect severe stomach upsets if I overheated, and another that Karachi sun didn't turn you golden, but grey. I chose to ignore them.

Eventually, though, I gave up, oppressed by the heat, and went inside, hoping that noone would gloat about my failed mission. When I'd cooled down, we went for a driving tour of the city, my aunt, my mother, and I. My aunt pointed out places of their childhood – the house where they had lived as children, the place where this cousin or that cousin still lived. Mum repeated that she couldn't believe the change. As we passed the building where she'd gone to school, she told me that, when she grew up, there was nothing but marshland between this structure and the sea, where now a thousand buildings had sprung up.

A few days later, we went for dinner with an old family friend at Bar-B-Que Tonite, a five-floor restaurant with a roof terrace offering a spectacular view of the city by night. It was a balmy evening, the heat of the day lifting to a near-perfect temperature after the sun went down, the breeze a reminder of the nearby sea.

We looked out over Karachi, the lights shining under the haze of pollution. 'I can't get my bearings at all,' said Mum.

It was a running theme of the fortnight we spent there. After four decades of exponential expansion and change in the city, she couldn't get her head around the elaborate network of roads, the irrational grid system of the Defence Housing Authority (DHA), the upmarket suburb where we were staying, the multitude of buildings covering the earth she instinctively loved and, most of all, the men with guns everywhere. My mother's city was no longer her city, and it was under siege.

◆

Two weeks later, we were back at Karachi airport. We went through a mind-boggling number of security checks; a metal detector and scanner at the entrance, again at check-in, then yet again at the baggage drop.

As we went through to departures and I waited to put my handbag through a scanner for the fourth or fifth time, a woman clad head to toe in black – down to black gloves and a black face covering – pushed in front of me. Outraged by this clear violation of queuing etiquette, I was about to protest, when Mum touched my arm. 'It's not worth it,' she said. 'Queues aren't important here. We'll be back in England soon.'

I set off the metal detector when I walked through it, so was taken into a small cubicle, where a woman in uniform scanned my body with a handheld metal detector. She eyed me suspiciously. 'You Pakistani, Ma'am?'

'Yes, my mother is Pakistani,' I said, arms spread wide.

'You don't look Pakistani,' she said, and waved me out of the room. The offhand comment felt cutting. After two weeks in a family setting, unquestioningly accepted, it was a sharp reminder that I looked different. I thought of all the times I'd been asked in the UK where I was 'actually' from and wondered, with a momentary sense of complete exhaustion, if I would ever fit anywhere.

I found Mum and we wandered over to the gate, where we sat listening to announcements.

'Please remain seated until your seat number is called,' said a voice over the tannoy, in English and then in Urdu.

About 80 per cent of the other people sitting at the gate stood up and charged towards the desk.

'I hate Pakistanis,' said Mum, looking despairingly at the crowd of people amassed at the front.

I laughed, amused but also concerned someone might have heard. 'But Mum – they're your people.'

'I know,' she sighed. 'Why do you think I never come back?'

I left Karachi with more questions than answers. What was this country about, and what was my place in it? How could I at once be so accepted and so marked out? Why was it that certain aspects of the culture seemed so natural to me and other elements so baffling? I'd spent a lifetime in the UK more or less defined by my difference, my exotic other half of ethnicity – but did that really mean anything?

It was loosely that enigma which brought me back there, eighteen months later. Riven by militancy, but also about to undergo its first-ever democratic transition from one civilian government to another, Pakistan was in the throes of an identity crisis of its own. It was almost always characterised in the press as a basket-case, an unstable ally that was exporting terror. But I knew from my own experience that this was a gross oversimplification of this gigantic, beautiful country.

After going straight from school to university to work, all within England's southeast, I'd been plagued by itchy feet for years. This nagging anxiety about where I fitted in was the final push. In defiance of warnings about the free-fall of the British media, I handed in my notice and booked a flight. I spent a year there in all, working, travelling, figuring out my place in this complicated land and putting back together the two 'halves' of my identity, halves I hadn't realised were fractured. I've been back every year since. It's not home, but there is a place for me.

Sabrina Mahfouz

Battleface

Camilla (a journalist) and Ablah (a cosmetic doctor specialising in facial rejuvenation) are having an interview chat in a spare room at Ablah's clinic.

ABLAH: I'd estimate you're thirty-three years old, from the depth of the fountain of lines between your eyebrows. You take your job extremely seriously, working until the light late hours – revealed by the shade of dark skin under your eyes. You haven't been joyously happy for a while – the laughter lines around your mouth don't match your age. You don't eat well. You drink too much coffee. It gives you palpitations, but you drink it anyway because – because of this dedication to your work. And there's something else, something I can't quite put my finger on.

You'd have to sit under my lamp for a proper analysis.

CAMILLA: Wow. That was – amazing. I feel… naked.

ABLAH: Accurate, then?

CAMILLA: I had no idea all that was right here, on my face.

ABLAH: Most don't.

CAMILLA: So you really are the best.

ABLAH: Well, no – maybe, one of.

CAMILLA: Why do you do what you do, Ablah?

ABLAH: I love it.

CAMILLA: What exactly do you love about it?

ABLAH: The possibility.

CAMILLA: Possibility?

ABLAH: When a client comes to see me, they're hoping to rediscover their possibility. It's a beautiful thing to be able to help them do that.

CAMILLA: How *do* you do that?

ABLAH: I allow time to be pulled back inside a person's being.

CAMILLA: Quite a feat.

ABLAH: When they look in the mirror, they no longer see trauma, or disappointment, just…

CAMILLA: Possibility?

ABLAH: Exactly.

CAMILLA: So in a way, medical facial rejuvenation is like… therapy?

ABLAH: Yes, except cheaper, faster and far more effective. Trust me on that.

CAMILLA: I will.

ABLAH: And how about you Camilla, why did you become a journalist?

CAMILLA: To meet the most interesting minds I possibly could without having one myself.

ABLAH: An unfair assessment, I'm sure. I always felt the world could be changed with words.

CAMILLA: Do you write?

ABLAH: I did. Years ago. Just… silly things, really.

CAMILLA: Like what?

ABLAH: Poetry, mainly. I was an angry young woman!

CAMILLA: What were you angry about?

ABLAH: The world being so far from what I wanted it to be.

CAMILLA: What did you want it to be?

ABLAH: It was just… the usual stuff you feel before reality and responsibility take over.

CAMILLA: No poetry any more then?

ABLAH: No time for that, probably quite fortunately.

CAMILLA: Do you find time to do anything outside of work?

ABLAH: Hardly, it's non-stop these days.

CAMILLA: I suppose the Best Botox Award helped with that?

ABLAH: Maybe, but demand for these procedures has been increasing steadily for a long time.

CAMILLA: Why do you think that is?

ABLAH: Hope. Despair. People need to be in control of something. Plain old vanity. So many reasons.

CAMILLA: Do you miss cardiology?

ABLAH: Um. Well. I haven't asked myself that question for a long time.

CAMILLA: Perhaps that means no, then?

ABLAH: Actually, I probably do. The urgency of it, the absolute life or death of it – that, maybe I miss that.

CAMILLA: I imagine it must be quite something, to save a life?

ABLAH: There's nothing else that even comes close.

CAMILLA: So why did you leave?

ABLAH: It was hard, as a single parent. The night shifts, the emergencies. Cosmetics was more manageable, back then.

CAMILLA: And more lucrative I bet?

ABLAH: That side was appreciated too, but it took a long while to get this clinic to where it is today.

CAMILLA: What about your family now?

ABLAH: What about them?

CAMILLA: Do you get to spend time with them?

ABLAH: Not… as much as I'd like.

CAMILLA: Are they proud of the reputation you've achieved?

ABLAH: I hope so. Sorry, how much longer do you—

CAMILLA: Not long, I know you're busy. I really appreciate your time.

ABLAH: No problem.

CAMILLA: You said you have children?

ABLAH: I have a son.

Pause.

CAMILLA: Nasim.

ABLAH: Yes, Nasim. How do you – how do you know that?

CAMILLA: I met him.

ABLAH: You met him? Where?

CAMILLA: At a party.

ABLAH: But how did you know – how did you make the connection –

CAMILLA: He told me all about his famous Botox doctor mother from Shepherd's Bush, it had to be you.

ABLAH: He told you about me?

CAMILLA: You sound surprised.

ABLAH: I – we… we've had a…

CAMILLA: He mentioned things have been a bit difficult.

ABLAH: To say the least.

CAMILLA: He also said things are looking up, between you.

ABLAH: You had quite an in depth chat for a party, then?

CAMILLA: It was a Ministry party, for those who'd served in Iraq.

Pause. Ablah takes this in.

ABLAH: And what would a journalist for a high-end lifestyle magazine be doing at such a party?

Pause. This is the opening for Camilla to reveal herself. Change of tone, etc.

CAMILLA: Ablah, the reason I need to speak to you today is far more important than to write a feature /on you –

ABLAH: You're not writing a feature on me?

CAMILLA: No, I'm not.

Pause.

ABLAH: What exactly are we doing here then?

CAMILLA: We need to discuss something very important with you.

ABLAH: 'We'? I can only see you, here, Camilla. What is this, what do you want?

CAMILLA: World peace and national security.

ABLAH: How sweet.

CAMILLA: I'm serious, Ablah.

ABLAH: You're not a journalist.

CAMILLA: No.

ABLAH: Who are you?

CAMILLA: You'll always know me as Camilla.

ABLAH: I really dislike games. At school, I used to pretend I had my period every single week in order to avoid playing any kind of game.

CAMILLA: Funny. PE was my favourite subject. Always thought I'd grow up to be a runner.

Look, I apologise for the underhand method to get you

talking to me. We just find it's easier than an unexpected knock at the door.

ABLAH: 'We', who is this 'we'?

CAMILLA: We need you, Ablah. We need your talent and we need your insight, nobody else will do.

ABLAH: Again, oh my, I'm not understanding exactly who 'we' is?

CAMILLA: I work for a section, a special section, of the Ministry.

ABLAH: The ministry as in *the* ministry?

CAMILLA: We've been searching for someone who fits your profile for a while now.

ABLAH: *My* profile? The ministry? I mean—

CAMILLA: When Nasim mentioned you I—

ABLAH: Just hold. The hell. Up. I don't even know where to begin with—

CAMILLA: I understand it's a bit of a shock, but your cooperation is paramount to—

ABLAH: Shock? I thought I was spending my lunch hour being interviewed by *Gun* magazine for God's sake and now it's – I don't know, what is this?

CAMILLA: As I was saying, when Nasim mentioned you I—

ABLAH: That, that there, I just – When you say Nasim mentioned me, do you mean he just mentioned me, as in passing conversational mentioned, or do you mean mentioned me as in…

CAMILLA: Conversational only. He doesn't know about this meeting.

ABLAH: What – why was he even *at* a Ministry party? He didn't 'serve' in Iraq, he was a bloody mercenary.

CAMILLA: We couldn't survive without them these days, Ablah, although nobody says mercenary any more, it's private security mostly.

ABLAH: Oh well, in that case...

CAMILLA: The best of them become, well, good friends with the Ministry.

ABLAH: Nasim has left all that behind now.

CAMILLA: I'm here to talk about you...

ABLAH: So what – what the hell is this 'profile' of mine exactly?

CAMILLA: I'm going to give you as much information as I can.

ABLAH: That would be appreciated, information, that would be good.

CAMILLA: Do you want some water?

ABLAH: This is my bloody office! If I want some water I'll get some water.

CAMILLA: Of course.

ABLAH: I'm not even sure why you're still in here, actually. I should just ask you to leave.

CAMILLA: I'm sure you'd like to know what I have to say.

ABLAH: *I'm* sure that whatever you say will be a load of bullshit.

CAMILLA: Look, I completely understand your slight hostility to the Ministry, perhaps even to this country, but what we—

ABLAH: Ha, *slight* hostility? Surely, in a 'special section' you do your research before you ambush someone?

CAMILLA: You don't have Facebook.

ABLAH: Are you serious?

CAMILLA: These days it's tricky when someone has no personal online presence.

ABLAH: World-class intelligence.

CAMILLA: All we could find was an article written when you were a student, arguing the Palestinian case against Israeli expansionism.

ABLAH: And from that you couldn't surmise how I'd feel about being approached by a government that still supports such actions all these decades later?

CAMILLA: You're a famous cosmetic doctor specialising in facial rejuvenation. It doesn't scream socialist. Getting older makes us see things differently.

ABLAH: Not things like apartheid and occupation, Camilla.

CAMILLA: What we need you for is so significant to our strategy, Ablah, we are willing to overlook any ideological differences. I hope that gives you an indication of how important this is?

Ablah settles a little. Feels more in control again now. Looks at her watch.

ABLAH: Well you better get on with it then, my PA will be welcoming my next clients soon.

CAMILLA: Have you heard of the upward trend in cosmetic facial treatments in Iraq, particularly in Baghdad?

ABLAH: I'm aware.

CAMILLA: The relative rate of treatments is outnumbering those even in America.

ABLAH: And?

CAMILLA: Every woman who can afford it – and a few men – are Botoxing and peeling and nose-jobbing their way out of decades of despair.

ABLAH: Poetic, your point?

CAMILLA: You said yourself, what you do is better than therapy.

ABLAH: I believe so.

CAMILLA: Your fellow Iraqis *(Ablah rolls her eyes at this phrasing)* obviously agree, there's only four registered psychiatrists in Baghdad – *but* 344 people are licensed to administer Botox.

ABLAH: A license doesn't mean they have a clue what they're

doing.

CAMILLA: Exactly!

Camilla is excited that Ablah has said this. Ablah scrutinises her.

ABLAH: Oh god, do you want me – no, you/ can't be –

CAMILLA: We want you to run a clinic, just like this one, but in Baghdad.

ABLAH: I don't want to run a clinic in Baghdad.

CAMILLA: You'll be in stratospheric demand – the best Botox doctor in London *and* she's Iraqi, perfect.

ABLAH: Again. Slowly. I – don't – want – to – run a clinic – in Baghdad. I'm very happy in Shepherd's Bush, thank you.

CAMILLA: As you know, clients talk when they have treatments. They're nervous, it's intimate, they *talk*. ISIS have a stronghold there, in Iraq and we—

ABLAH: Camilla, I get it. You want me to *spy* for you? For Her Majesty's Government?

CAMILLA: We want you to provide the unrivalled service and skills you do here, whilst encouraging those who come to see you to… let you in to their personal lives a little.

ABLAH: Their personal lives… and details of planned suicide attacks they might just blurt out in the middle of me injecting their epidermis?

CAMILLA: Nobody else can do this.

ABLAH: How do you know?

CAMILLA: We run a training centre out there. Two hundred students per year. The best teachers. And still, not one—

ABLAH: A training centre for spies who can do Botox?

CAMILLA: A training centre for cosmetic surgery and aesthetic treatments.

ABLAH: An official cosmetic surgery training centre run by British intelligence in Iraq?

CAMILLA: It's run by a quanco, of course, there's no official link to intelligence at all, but it's no secret that the UK Government support it.

ABLAH: I've never heard of it.

CAMILLA: Cosmetic surgery is an important industry in a post-conflict locality.

ABLAH: *Post-* conflict?

CAMILLA: Well, officially. Look, we encourage anything that subverts the political rhetoric and the idea that women should cover themselves. We want them to feel free.

ABLAH: Whilst spying on them?

CAMILLA: We only want to know more about certain women, not average citizens.

ABLAH: What you've said, you know, it shows how nothing's changed.

CAMILLA: Meaning?

ABLAH: The level of knowledge you have of Iraqi life, after all this time. It's still superficial and insufficient. Women can get their noses hacked away and their faces frozen to the ice age but they'll stay covered and if they don't, that doesn't make them more free – you must know that?

CAMILLA: We don't have the data.

ABLAH: God, you don't need data Camilla, you just need eyes.

CAMILLA: We need your eyes.

Ablah, exhausted, needs to put this to bed.

ABLAH: Have you read the Chilcot Report?

CAMILLA: An abridged version, yes.

ABLAH: Don't you feel ashamed?

CAMILLA: I was very junior at that time. And, I believe our advice wasn't listened to, intelligence agencies weren't to blame.

ABLAH: So what's the point?

CAMILLA: Of?

ABLAH: Of what you do, of what you're asking me to do, if nobody listens when it matters anyway?

CAMILLA: Many of the top minds behind ISIS are female. Wives of the cabinet being our main interest area at the moment.

ABLAH: And miraculously, out of the 345 ones available, they'll go to see a Botox doctor newly arrived from London?

CAMILLA: They have to maintain a high status within their groups and a high status as a woman is impossible to maintain without a ferocious approach to anti-ageing, as you'll know. They will want the best.

ABLAH: It is funny.

CAMILLA: What?

ABLAH: I've wanted to be in a room with one of you people for so long and now here I am and I can't even catch my thoughts—

CAMILLA: We're conscious of the fact we've made plenty of mistakes when it comes to Iraq—

ABLAH: Mistakes!?

CAMILLA: That's why we're pursuing non-traditional routes into finding out what we can about those intent on destroying innocent lives.

ABLAH: Innocent lives. I wonder what you mean by innocent.

CAMILLA: I mean people who aren't planning to attack other people.

ABLAH: Do you know anyone who died there?

CAMILLA: Yes. My partner. She was twenty-three.

ABLAH: I am sorry to hear that. Truly.

CAMILLA: The company who made the armour for the vehicle she was in made some redundancies to save costs. They didn't realise they'd got rid of everyone who knew how to fit the armour.

ABLAH: And yet, you carried on?

CAMILLA: Ablah, I can't stand here and give you a speech on the magnificence of the monarchy and the righteousness of our military interventions. I know plenty of them, but – that's not why I do this.

ABLAH: You believe you can make a difference? Save some lives?

CAMILLA: I know I can, I do. The work we do, it saves lives, it keeps at least some people safe, we just can't make a poster out of it.

ABLAH: I arrived here when I was fifteen. We literally walked through flames to find ourselves here, in Shepherd's Bush. It wasn't as friendly then as it is now, not as easy to find a piece of home. My mother didn't speak any more. She'd refused to leave Iraq earlier. My sister and my brother, younger than me, twelve and ten. Small, sweet faces, big eyes. They were the cherished ones. I was arrogant, precocious, rebellious. The two little ones were cheeky but adoring of my parents. They loved doing anything for them. In Iraq, one day, they went out to the market for my mother, she'd ran out of the cheese my father lived for. I was sulking, listening to music, doodling the name of a boy I had a crush on all over my schoolbooks. Life continues as much as it can, even when it has been deemed worthless by those in buildings like the one where you work.

We all heard the explosion. So quick. Like a pillowcase being ripped in half whilst you sleep on it. Then the falling. A sprinkling, really. Bricks and limbs and pipes and poles falling so softly, like raindrops from where we stood, searching with our eyes. We couldn't see the damage, only hear it. We stood frozen outside the house, me, my mother and father, wishing our ears to be wrong, wishing to see their small, sweet faces running to us, laughing that they'd played a trick, they'd made us think we were in a film, here is the cheese, baba, here is a kiss, 'ammi, here is a hug, big sister.

We had to wrap parts of their little bodies together in a white cloth because we didn't know who was who.

My father said we had to go then, at least to save me, the uncherished child who was now the only child and so, cherished, a little. My mother didn't argue because she didn't speak. We made our awkward, painful, silent way here, to you and I was glad, I really was. I flourished.

CAMILLA: What about your mother?

ABLAH: To lose children, there's no coming back from that.

CAMILLA: It must be… horrific.

ABLAH: So many children have died in Iraq. All over. So many, still dying. Small bodies, the cloth for five of them can be made from one adult's shroud. If they can even be found, to be buried. War, Camilla, does not keep any people 'safe'.

Pause. Ablah is upset. Camilla is momentarily saddened by this accusation of failure on her part.

CAMILLA: I know we're asking a lot from you, Ablah and we wouldn't do so unless—

ABLAH: Did Nasim tell you why we've had a difficult relationship?

CAMILLA: No, he didn't.

ABLAH: I hadn't spoken to him for five years until two months ago.

CAMILLA: Five years is a long time.

ABLAH: To not speak to your only child? It's a lifetime.

CAMILLA: Because he went to Iraq?

ABLAH: Despite all my stories, all my ranting to him against the war machine, despite never having heard a 'hello' from his Grandma, never being able to meet his uncle and aunty, he still decided the money was too good to say no to. To privately patrol a prison camp. For the British Army. Unthinkable. Indigestible. I – well, everything is a failure after that.

CAMILLA: He came back safe.

ABLAH: Thank God, *he* did. Who knows what happened to those he patrolled… But now that I'm talking to him again, trying, trying to untangle how we could hold such opposing views on such fundamental matters, squeezing out the love in my heart to cover the scars of sorrow he caused me – I simply cannot step away from him to do what you're asking me to, even if I wanted to. Do you understand Camilla? I won't leave my son again.

Pause.

CAMILLA: I had hoped to tell you this once you'd agreed, as a pleasant surprise of sorts. I hadn't anticipated such…

ABLAH: What, tell me what?

CAMILLA: Nasim is… He's working for us now.

ABLAH: No. No.

CAMILLA: He's been through the recruitment process, all the vetting, the training.

ABLAH: You fucking… you stood there and knew… he told me he was working on writing, he was going on a… course—

CAMILLA: He's legally obliged to not reveal where he works, of course.

ABLAH: What is he going to be doing—

CAMILLA: I can't tell you—

ABLAH: Bullshit, you've just told me more than you should anyway. So tell me.

CAMILLA: He… he's due to be deployed to Baghdad, soon.

Pause.

ABLAH: For how long?

CAMILLA: Two months, to begin with.

ABLAH: To begin with?

CAMILLA: He has a lot of talent, very promising.

ABLAH: You vultures!

CAMILLA: Ablah—

ABLAH: How can you do this to people? You know what it feels like to lose someone senselessly, or was that all just a lie to get me talking—

CAMILLA: That was the truth.

ABLAH: And yet – and yet – are you even human?

CAMILLA: This is what I can do. To make the world I want to see.

ABLAH: Why did you tell me about Nasim?

CAMILLA: I was always planning to. I just thought it would be under… more favourable circumstances.

ABLAH: Are you able to stop his deployment? Do you have that authority?

CAMILLA: I can't stop him being deployed. I could certainly cite conflict of interests – if you were going to be there, of course – and push that he's sent elsewhere or given a London-based desk job for a while.

ABLAH: Desk job. You must give him a desk job.

CAMILLA: I can only do that if the conflict of interest is there – you.

ABLAH: If I say yes, when will I become… active?

CAMILLA: Next week, ideally. We have the clinic ready, the timing is crucial, for reasons I can't tell you yet, until you sign.

ABLAH: Will he know?

CAMILLA: He's still junior. He won't be cleared to that level. We'll come up with a reason.

ABLAH: My God, my God. How did this happen? Would you be able to guarantee he would never be deployed to Iraq?

CAMILLA: For as long as I'm employed by the Ministry, yes. Beyond that, no.

Pause.

CAMILLA: I'm aware you need to get back to work soon.

ABLAH: Yes.

CAMILLA: But this is quite urgent, due to the—

ABLAH: Crucial timing?

CAMILLA: Yes.

ABLAH: If I say no?

CAMILLA: We really hope you won't.

ABLAH: If I do?

CAMILLA: Nasim will go to Baghdad…

ABLAH: And?

CAMILLA: And counter-terrorism measures have become pretty comprehensive these days.

ABLAH: You'd arrest me?

CAMILLA: We could.

ABLAH: Would you? Really?

CAMILLA: There's been a lot of arrests. For women with… your background.

ABLAH: I take it you don't mean in medicine.

CAMILLA: The first person to be convicted under the updated anti-terrorism legislation was a Muslim woman who wrote poetry.

ABLAH: Poetry?

CAMILLA: About decapitation and various, worryingly violent things.

ABLAH: Ever read *American Psycho*? Bret Easton Ellis?

CAMILLA: I'm not saying I agree, I'm saying it's not as difficult as you may think.

ABLAH: If you look like me, you mean? So the 'terror poet' has been taken. Would I be the 'Botox bomber'?

CAMILLA: Who knows what would happen, but the slightest incident wouldn't be good for business, would it?

ABLAH: You'd be surprised, Camilla, not everybody shares your love of Queen and country.

CAMILLA: It must have been difficult, growing up.

ABLAH: How do you mean?

CAMILLA: In a country you're not from. Viewed with hatred at worst, pity at best. Unspoken suspicion of deserving your fate following you around.

ABLAH: I told you, I flourished here.

CAMILLA: You had to, you're a survivor. But they didn't make it easy, did they?

ABLAH: Nothing in life is easy.

CAMILLA: At school, being the refugee kid, the one nobody wanted to sit next to, the one nobody spoke to, the one who had to learn the language quick enough to pass tests all the other kids had been preparing for since they were born. The one nobody chose for their team at PE — is that why you hated it so much?

ABLAH: This is beneath even you.

CAMILLA: Proving your worth, proving you could do it, do anything you wanted, do better than they all could — that's what got you out of bed every day. That's what gave you the strength to look at your silent mother and tell her about your day as if she'd asked.

ABLAH: Stop it.

CAMILLA: Nobody to believe in you, everyone to expect nothing from you. The reserves of belief you must have buried inside you, Ablah, it's incredible.

ABLAH: You do not know me.

CAMILLA: Every step you made you had to justify why you were allowed to take it before you could make the next one.

You had to laugh at jokes that broke your heart at first until, you got so used to it, you started making them yourself.

ABLAH: I'm not sure I've made who I am clear enough—

CAMILLA: You had to be validated at every stage by someone else – a man, someone who'd already made it, someone trusted, someone British, someone white. From school to college to uni to hospitals to clinics—

ABLAH: What is your point, Camilla, just shut up and tell me! What is your goddamn point?!

CAMILLA: I could make it all unhappen, Ablah. All that work. A lifetime of work. Of sacrifice, of soul-destroying boundary bending. A high-profile arrest. Rumours. Association with unfavourables from back home. It would be so easy for us, so utterly, boringly easy that it makes me feel nauseous, to be honest. Because I admire you and I would hate to have to do that to someone of your conviction and strength.

Ablah is very upset – this is unbearable.

ABLAH: But you would.

CAMILLA: I would.

ABLAH: Your dedication is exemplary.

CAMILLA: You have a real opportunity here, Ablah.

ABLAH: Yes, perhaps I do.

CAMILLA: Okay?

Camilla is searching for her answer. Ablah takes her time.

ABLAH: Do you know that botulinum is the most toxic chemical in the world to humans? That Botox is a form of that, the very thing people pay to have injected into their faces?

CAMILLA: Yes, I'm aware. It's also one of the chemicals Saddam was suspected of stockpiling for biological warfare.

ABLAH: All those Iraqi women, hoping to find love, acceptance, some tingle of excitement again, something, anything, all with the help of the very thing that was used to justify the decimation of their lives, and the cosmetic use of it was invented by the country that orchestrated all that destruction. Irony doesn't begin to cover it.

CAMILLA: It is what it is.

ABLAH: Did you choose Nasim for his role, just so you could get me?

CAMILLA: No. He applied a long time ago. It was just lucky, that he mentioned what you did.

ABLAH: Lucky for who?

CAMILLA: Like I said, this is an opportunity for someone of your… passion.

Pause. Is Camilla encouraging Ablah to cause trouble?

Ablah is really struggling with what to do.

Camilla checks her phone/watch.

CAMILLA: Ablah?

ABLAH: I know how to kill.

CAMILLA: There won't be any killing.

ABLAH: There's always killing.

CAMILLA: Not for you.

ABLAH: For the drones? For Nasim?

CAMILLA: This is about saving lives, not taking them, isn't it?

Camilla is almost looking for Ablah's validation on this point.

ABLAH: If I was to open a tiny, undiluted bottle of botulinum – which is luckily very easy for someone like me to come by – and put it here, between us, the airborne particles from this deadly toxin would likely kill us both relatively quickly, perhaps before my PA, sitting just out there, came knocking. I wonder though, if one of us had significant exposure to Botox already, they might outlive the other long enough to get help for themselves, just in time.

CAMILLA: But you don't have that tiny bottle, do you Ablah?

ABLAH: It's all about possibility, isn't it, Camilla?

BLACKOUT.

Hanan al-Shaykh

An Eye That Sees

A voice rang out, loud and tuneful, through the Victoria and Albert Museum. The visitors froze, puzzled – they had never heard such a strange melody. They reacted as though a bird had just landed on their heads.

It was the attendant. He stood in the middle of the gallery, his eyes closed, his head swaying from side to side, his hands clutching his heart as though afraid it might fly away. Usually a shadowy presence, a figure of unobtrusive authority, suddenly appeared before them as a man of flesh and blood.

◆

In his early days at the job, Tareq had heartily greeted each visitor as they entered, and had taken it upon himself to accompany them as they wandered around the gallery. But before long his supervisor had asked him to keep his distance: people had complained of feeling followed, monitored. He was to stay in his corner and only intervene if there was a specific reason; to ask someone to lower their voice, silence their mobile phone, refrain from leaning against the exhibits or put away their sandwiches. On the whole he complied, except for the odd moment when he couldn't resist telling an old man that he reminded him of an uncle back home, or remarking on the coldness of the weather.

When he had first come to Britain, ten years before, Tareq would invariably introduce himself by telling the story of Tareq ibn Ziyad, the general who had led the Islamic conquest of Andalusia, and after whom both he and the mountain of Gibraltar were named. Years of seeing eyes glaze over went by before he finally understood that the British didn't care, and he stopped taking such pride in his name.

In the face of this indifference he tried to content himself, instead, with the fact that his one dream of a life in Britain had, at least, come true. He had grown up hearing his father and the village elders speak with envy about those who had left Yemen and made a life for themselves in Europe or the Arabian Gulf. Time and time again, he heard them say, *a young man who stays in this country won't find a thing to eat but flies; won't even find a shroud to cover him when they lay him to rest in the earth.* Tareq had escaped this fate. He had left his job at the Yemeni airline in Sanaa after talking to a customer who boasted to Tareq that he could earn in just a few days in the UK what amounted to Tareq's monthly salary in Yemen. The last ticket Tareq issued was his own.

After a great deal of effort he had managed to secure the necessary papers and was awarded leave to remain in the UK – and permission to work. He began drifting from job to job – from a metals factory in Sheffield to a hospital in Hackney – until his Egyptian flatmate suggested he try his luck at the V&A, where he himself worked as a handyman, hanging pictures and moving objects to and from storage.

The position came to him on a plate of gold, as they would have said at home, and Tareq became a museum attendant. It was a neat, respectable job, and he was proud that it meant he didn't need to work with his hands: as far as those back home were concerned, this was as good as being a company director. Besides, the role offered plenty of time for quiet contemplation. Over the course of the following months he reduced himself, as requested, to a set of ears and a pair of eyes.

Tareq busied himself with adding and subtracting, comparing his earnings and expenses, brooding over what he wanted to buy, and what he had bought and regretted. He calculated the sum he had left over to send to his parents in Yemen, and thought of the special massage chair that might help ease his father's rheumatism. Would it be possible to ship it over? And if so, how would they manage to squeeze it along the narrow alleyway leading to their home – or, for that matter, through the tiny front door?

Should he go home for the holidays, he wondered? There were rumours things in Yemen were becoming more unstable – might they become so dangerous that they would shut down flights altogether? Perhaps he should devote some of his time off to finding a bride instead. His Somali friend Ahmed, a bus driver, had told him about a promising young woman he'd met who was single. She worked at a post office and greeted him ever so politely as she got on the bus every day. If he weren't married himself, Ahmed said, he'd be tempted to ask for her hand.

Tareq didn't get to meet anyone through work. The women at the museum – employees and visitors alike, whether foreigners or Arabs – came from a completely different world. They were the sort of women who walked around in spindly heels that looked like the twigs Tareq used to clean his teeth. He could sooner reach the stars than talk to a woman like that. Life here was expensive, too. Even a sip of water came at a price.

His Egyptian friend bemoaned the fact that the V&A was not more like the antiquities museums in Cairo. If you worked there, he claimed, you could make double your wages by hustling the tourists. Threaten them with grave consequences if they take a photograph, then whisper that you're willing to turn a blind eye should they extend you a handful of cash. Or if you spot someone with a keen interest in mummies, offer to show her some 'special specimens' that are not on public display, then lead her to a back room housing a few bird or dog remains.

Today his train of thought had been abruptly derailed when a woman with familiar features had entered the museum, followed by a television crew. She walked up to one of the paintings on display and contemplated it briefly before turning to the camera. A man handed her a microphone and proceeded to ask her a question in English. She answered in classical Arabic, but a few words slipped out in Yemeni dialect. Tareq inched closer to hear.

'When I was a little girl, there was one mirror in our house. I would gaze into it for hours. My mother tried to wrest me away. She used to say, "If you keep this up, that mirror will swallow you whole!" One day I was helping her bake some bread and I spilled a little salt – she was furious. She slapped me, hard, and said, "On the Day of Judgement, God will make you pick these grains up, one by one, with your eyelashes!" and it was that threat, that gloating threat, that made hot tears rush to my eyes, and not the slap at all.

'I stared long and hard at those grains through blurry eyes. Slowly my vision cleared and I burst out: "If God is so big and has to take care of the whole universe all the time, will he really be so worried about a few spilled grains of salt?"

'A realisation began to crystallise within me. I began to understand why I kept gazing into the mirror that way. I was asserting my right to look, *really* look: to delve into the world around me and ask questions, even if those questions made people turn away in anger or apathy or fear – questions big and small, about boys and girls, about our life and traditions, about nature and the meaning of it all. Once, when I had been repeatedly shushed, I found myself yelling, not only at my mother, but at everyone, including my youngest sister, who was in the garden playing with one of our goats, "Why are we created with eyes, then? Isn't it so we can see?" And with the greatest urgency I rushed to draw an eye, as if it were a matter of life or death.

'That eye sought to expose what others tried to obscure, what everyone tried to hide from me for fear that I would break the rules, step outside the bounds of the familiar. But the tighter the chokehold on me grew, the more I rebelled by drawing eyes everywhere: on my hands, on my legs, on my clothes and schoolbooks, on the chairs and walls and bedspreads.'

Tareq's heart began to hammer in his chest. He almost cried out, 'I know you! I know who you are! You're Aisha!'

The Englishman broke in with another question. 'Why do you use henna in your paintings? Are oils not available in Yemen?'

The painter smiled. 'Painting materials are available in the capital, Sanaa. But henna is an essential part of my culture and upbringing, of our daily rituals. Plus I find it has beautiful colours… and a powerful, evocative smell.'

The attendant's trembling heart could not resist coming closer and closer to the woman from his homeland, to the girl he had once seen squatting in the dirt fifteen years ago. It was said, at the time, that she had lost her mind, mixing henna incessantly and painting eyes, day and night, on anything within reach, even rocks and trees. One neighbour warned the others not to hang their clothes outside to dry, after coming out of her house to find her freshly laundered sheets staring back at her. Others whispered that the girl was possessed, she was not drawing eyes, but cryptic signs.

Tareq had been intrigued by these rumours. He recalled how he had made his way to her house on the outskirts of a neighbouring village. He wanted to lay his eyes on her, and if her beauty appealed to him, he had resolved to ask for her hand and break her free of the black magic. He remembered now how he found her scribbling eyes on pebbles and in the dirt, and when he crept closer she looked up, straight into his eyes. She had smiled and asked, 'Who are you?' In panic, he scrambled backwards and fled. A normal girl would never initiate a conversation with a boy like that! Once at a safe distance, he looked over his shoulder to see her mother dragging her back into the house and raining down blows. When he later heard that she had disappeared – run away, or maybe been killed? – he blamed himself terribly that he hadn't whisked her away that day. But soon, leaving his village for the city, for university and a new life, he began to forget.

She looked younger than him now, tall and willowy, even though they were both in their thirties. The years had not been so kind to him: they had stripped away his hair and puffed up his paunch. How incomprehensibly strange that they should be here now in the land of the English, her mysterious eyes on display in a museum, revered as art, and he responsible for guarding it.

Tareq waited until she had finished her interview, then approached her, hand outstretched. 'I'm from Yemen – from your home town, actually. I just want to say that our pride in you is bigger than this museum. A thousand congratulations.'

She shook his hand, briefly. 'You're so lucky to be living in this oasis of knowledge and beauty,' she said politely. 'Or do you get tired of seeing the same things every day?'

An image of Tipu's Tiger, sinking its teeth into a British soldier, sprang to mind. The wooden statue with its striped tail was the one piece that had caught his attention since he started working at the museum six years ago, not least because on the tiger's face were inscribed the Arabic words *asad Allah,* 'the lion of God'. The tiger once used to produce horrifying mechanical shrieks and moans. More than once he had seen little children squirming out of their parents' grasp to run to it delightedly.

'No, I don't get bored – I move to a different room every day! Anyway, my name is Tareq and I'd be very happy to take you on a special tour of the museum, and maybe show you some of the things that are not on display. My colleague is in charge of the warehouse. Do you live in London? Let me give you my number.'

'No, I live in Aden – I'm just visiting.' He watched her press the digits into her mobile phone.

'Bye, Tareq.' As she smiled and shook his hand, he realised he would never hear from her.

He found himself standing alone in front of her painting. It was bigger than all the others. In the centre of the canvas was an eye the size of the earth. The smell of henna suddenly filled his nostrils. *Hanoon,* they called it in Yemen: 'she of the tender heart'. A familiar scene from his childhood crept unbidden into his mind: his mother filling a large tub with hot water and henna and submerging herself in it, her skin turning from white to gold.

The eye drew him in, and he basked in the warmth of the Yemeni sun. Its veins were the tremors on a heart monitor, inscriptions in Aisha's secret language. He read: *The eye is the gateway to the soul; the eye is insight; the eye is exploration. The ignorant are blind even if they see; the learned see even if they are blind.*

He understood now that those villagers had been right, in a way: Aisha *was* enchanted, enchanting. As he wandered from one room to another with Aisha's eye, he saw the treasures of the museum anew. Its pupil, crimson, like life-pumping blood, led him through an oasis of knowledge and beauty, to look and explore, to feel and wonder – and to remember.

The antique gilded candelabra were the flickering fireflies that dotted the Yemeni night. The ivory comb was the one his grandmother used to tug through his little sister's tangled hair. A sword of gold echoed the *janbiah* – the curved dagger Yemeni men wore tucked into their belts.

Everything before him – hand-woven rugs and lush textiles, wood inlaid with mother of pearl, pottery engraved with delicate shapes – all this, which was considered part of western heritage, he had seen before in the homes and buildings and mosques of Yemen. Raphael's image of Jesus and the miraculous draught of fish rang distant bells: a parallel legend that told of answered sea-prayers of a Yemeni sheikh. When he saw a tiny box containing a replica of a skeleton to remind human beings of the day of reckoning; a coloured clay bowl to serve soup to a new mother moments after childbirth; a glass bottle that, if broken, would bury its owner under a hailstorm of disaster – he thought: 'So many countries scattered across the earth. How is it that folklore is almost one?'

Tareq heaved a sigh. An old song bubbled up from deep within, and he let it take him over:

Oh henna, dear henna, oh drops of morning dew –
My sweetheart's eyes are a window that lets the breeze
sing through…

A hand clamped down on his shoulder. He opened his eyes with a start to find his supervisor pulling him to a corner of the room, asking in hushed, harried tones, 'What's going on here?'

'Sorry, I… I don't know what happened… it's like the… I felt for the first time this place – it… it reminded me of home.'

'You still have to keep it together at all times. You know

very well how we react when a visitor raises their voice, don't you?'

'Yes. I ask them to stop, and call in security if necessary.'

'Alright then. So you know the rules.'

Translated by Wiam El-Tamami

Biographies

Leila Aboulela is a Sudanese author whose short stories and novels engage with themes of identity, migration and Islamic spirituality. Her work includes *The Translator* (1999), which was chosen as a Notable Book of the Year by the *New York Times*, *Minaret* (2005), and the short story *The Museum*, which was included in her collection *Coloured Lights* (2001), for which she was awarded the Caine Prize for African Writing in 2000. A number of her plays have been broadcast by the BBC, and her most recent novel, *The Kindness of Enemies*, was published in 2015. She now lives in Aberdeen.

Shaista Aziz is a former international aid worker, Al Jazeera journalist, writer, and stand-up comedian from Oxford. Publications to which she has regularly contributed include *The Guardian* and *The Globe and Mail*, and she is a frequent panel guest on BBC Radio specialising in current affairs. Aziz has performed stand-up across the UK, winning the King Gong open mic competition at the Manchester Comedy Store in 2010. In 2014 she presented the BBC Three documentary *A Nation Divided? The Charlie Hebdo Aftermath*, in which she explored cultural and religious polarisation in the wake of the infamous shooting.

Seema Begum is fifteen years old and lives in Tower Hamlets, London. She loves reading books and in particular romantic novels. Begum loves writing, and her favourite subject at school is English. She aspires to become a judge, and she also has a dream to write a poem that will one day be studied by students.

Selma Dabbagh is a British-Palestinian novelist, blogger, journalist and reviewer. Born in Scotland, she now lives in London. Her work engages with themes such as idealism, rootlessness and political engagement, and the impact of social conformity. Her debut novel, *Out of It* (2011), which follows a family's experience of besieged Gaza, was nominated for the Guardian Book of the Year in both 2011 and 2012. Her short stories have appeared in various anthologies and publications, and her radio play *The Brick* was broadcast by the BBC in 2014. Her second book, *We Are Here Now*, is due for publication in 2017.

Born in Pakistan and raised in Scotland, **Imtiaz Dharker** is a poet and documentary film-maker. She has published several collections, including *Purdah* (1989), *I speak for the devil* (2001), *The terrorist at my table* (2006) and, most recently, *Over the Moon* (2014). In recognition of her work, she was awarded the Queen's Gold Medal for Poetry in 2014. Much of her poetry explores themes of identity and gender politics, geographical and cultural displacement, and the ramifications of the culture of purdah. She is an accomplished artist, and her pen-and-ink drawings have been featured in ten solo exhibitions across the world, including India, Hong Kong and the UK.

Asma Elbadawi is a visual artist and spoken word poet from Bradford. Her work is often a means of exploring her Sudanese heritage, and poetry has been the medium through which she has negotiated dyslexia. She was recently chosen as one of the finalists of the Words First competition, a collaboration between BBC Radio 1Xtra and the Roundhouse. She holds an MA in Visual Arts, and is interested in pursuing the themes of belonging and identity through the interplays between art, performance and the written word.

Fadia Faqir is an award-winning novelist, playwright and short story writer. Her works have been published in eighteen countries and translated into fourteen languages, and include five novels, among them *Pillars of Salt, My Name is Salma* and *Willow Trees Don't Weep*. She is also the editor and co-translator of *In the House of Silence: Autobiographical Essays by Arab Women Writers* (1998) and was the senior editor of the Arab Women Writers series, for which she received the Women in Publishing 1995 New Venture Award. She was a member of the judging panel of Al-Multaqa Short Story Competition 2016. Fadia Faqir is an Honorary Fellow of St Mary's College and a Writing Fellow at St Aidan's College, Durham University, where she teaches creative writing. She is a co-founder of the Banipal Visiting Writer Fellowship.

Born in Pakistan, **Nafeesa Hamid** is a poet, playwright and spoken word artist from Birmingham. Her work engages with issues of mental health, domestic violence, gender, identity and culture. Hamid regularly performs in various locations in both the Midlands and London, and has established a monthly open-mic night and poetry workshop. Organisations that she has collaborated with include Apples and Snakes, Birmingham Museum and Art Gallery, mac birmingham and Beatfreeks. She is currently studying in Derby and is part of Mouthy

Poets, a collective of young artists and performers based in Nottingham.

Triska Hamid is a journalist and editor who has covered the Middle East for the past eight years. She was the winner of the Columbia University & Citi Journalism Excellence Award. Hamid works across multiple platforms and publications, such as *Vice* and *The Telegraph*, as well as being the Business Editor for *The National* in the UAE. She also occasionally writes poetry, and was a participant of the Royal Court's Young Writer's Programme.

Raised in Reading but living in Birmingham, **Aliyah Hasinah Holder** is a spoken word poet and creative producer. Her work explores the themes of heritage and representation, seeking to use art as a tool for social change. She has previously collaborated with various organisations and collectives, including Beatfreeks, the Southbank Centre, The Poetry Society and BBC 1Xtra. In 2015, she founded Herstory LIVE, an event combining histories with performance art to raise money for charitable causes. As part of spoken word duo A2 she is currently working on a Random Acts Film for Channel 4.

Amina Jama is a nineteen-year-old British-Somali poet based in London. In 2015–2016 she was one of BBC 1xtra's Final Six for the Words First program, creating work for BBC iPlayer and The Roundhouse. She wants to make her audience challenge what they think they know about poetry, and inspire th~ fall in love with words. She is part of sever=l Lond~ performing across the city.

Sabrina Mahfouz is a British Egypt¹ ..aywright, poet and screenwriter. She was awarded th~ ..ge First Award for her play *Chef,* and her play *Clean* r~ .erred to New York in 2014.

Her poetry has been performed and produced for TV, radio and film, including in the recent *Railway Nation: A Journey in Verse* on BBC2. Mahfouz has an essay in the award-winning *The Good Immigrant*, and has published eight plays with Bloomsbury Methuen. *How You Might Know Me* is her debut collection of poetry with Out-Spoken Press.

Aisha Mirza is a writer and counsellor from East London, now living in Brooklyn, New York. She is interested in body hair, madness and race. Mirza studies the impact of microaggressions (including forced hair removal) on the psyche of queer black and brown people. Her work has appeared in *The Guardian, The Independent, Black Girl Dangerous* and *openDemocracy*.

Miss L is an actress and the creator of Casting Call Woe, a site where she highlights the very worst of casting calls. She regularly writes about the trials of being an actress, and her work has featured on Buzzfeed and in *The Guardian* and *Grazia*.

Hibaq Osman is a twenty-two-year-old Somali writer born and raised in West London. She currently studies psychology and counselling at Roehampton University. In 2012 she won both the Brent Poetry Slam and the Roundhouse Poetry Slam. She is a member of the Burn After Reading collective, a community of young and emerging poets and writers founded and supported by Jacob Sam-La Rose and Jasmine Cooray in London. Her poetry pamphlet *A Silence You Can Carry* is published by Out-Spoken Press.

Born in Pakistan and raised in Canada, **Shazea Quraishi** is a poet, playwright and translator

of poems *The Courtesan's Reply*, published as a pamphlet in 2012, is voiced by a series of Indian courtesans, exploring the dynamics of relationships, sexuality and the gaze. Her first collection, *The Art of Scratching*, was released in 2015. Having received an award from the Artists' International Development Fund of the Arts Council England, she recently travelled to Pakistan to undertake research for a transgender character that will feature in her upcoming play, *The Jasmine Terrace*.

Samira Shackle is a freelance British journalist, writing mainly on politics, terrorism and gender with a particular focus on the Indian subcontinent. In 2016, the Words by Women Awards shortlisted Shackle in the Foreign Correspondent category and she was also longlisted in the New Voices category at the One World Media Awards. In 2015, Shackle was awarded the Richard Beeston bursary by *The Times* newspaper; and in 2014, she was selected as one of MHP's top thirty journalists under 30. Shackle writes for the *New Statesman*, *The Guardian*, *The Times*, *Vice* and *Deutsche Welle*, and is Assistant Editor of the *New Humanist* magazine.

Novelist, columnist and reviewer **Kamila Shamsie** was born in Pakistan in 1973 to a family of women writers. A Fellow of the Royal Society of Literature, Shamsie is the author of six novels, including *Kartography* (2002) and *Burnt Shadows* (2009), which was shortlisted for the Orange Prize for Fiction. Most recently, *A God in Every Stone* (2014) was shortlisted for the Baileys Prize, the Walter Scott Prize for Historical Fiction and the DSC Prize for South Asian Literature. In 2013, she was included in the *Granta* list of twenty best young British writers. She grew up in Karachi and now lives in London.

Hanan al-Shaykh is a Lebanese author of contemporary Arab women's literature. A novelist, short-story writer and playwright, she is one of the leading women writers in the Arab world. Her stories deal with women's role in society, the relationship between the sexes, and the institution of marriage. Her novels have been translated into multiple languages and include *One Thousand and One Nights* and *Women of Sand and Myrrh*.

Born in Cairo in 1950, **Ahdaf Soueif** is a novelist and political and cultural commentator,. She is the author of a range of both fiction and non-fiction publications, including the bestselling *The Map of Love* (1999), shortlisted for the Booker Prize for Fiction, and *Cairo: My City, Our Revolution* (2012), a personal account of the beginnings of the Egyptian Revolution. She is a Fellow of the Royal Society of Literature and a board member of The Egyptian Initiative for Personal Rights. In 2008, she launched the world's first Palestine Festival of Literature (PalFest), of which she is the Founding Chair.

Chimene Suleyman is a writer and poet from London, currently living in New York. Her debut poetry collection, *Outside Looking On* (2014), was included in the *Guardian*'s Best Book List of 2014. She regularly contributes to publications and organisations such as *The Independent* and *Media Diversified* concerning race and gender issues, and has performed at events and venues such as the Royal Festival Hall, the Bush Theatre, Secret Garden Party and OutSpoken. She was one of the contributors to the recently published *The Good Immigrant* (2016), a collection of essays exploring race and identity in contemporary Britain.

Azra Tabassum is a twenty-one-year-old English Litera student from Southhampton. Her debut poetry collecti *Shaking the Trees*, was published by Words Dance Publishing. Tabassum runs a popular poetry tumblr blog called *Hit the Body Like a Season*.

Credits

Leila Aboulela, *The Insider*, originally broadcast on BBC Radio 3, 2 November 2013.

Shaista Aziz, 'Blood and Broken Bodies', based on articles originally written for *The Guardian* and *The Globe and Mail*, 2014 and 2016 respectively.

Imtiaz Dharker, poems from *The Terrorist at My Table*, Bloodaxe Books, 2006. Reproduced with permission of Bloodaxe Books.

Fadia Faqir, 'Under the Cypress Tree', first published in *Wasafiri* special online issue, 2014. The short story was shortlisted for the 2010 Bridport Prize.

Triska Hamid, edited version of 'Islamic Tinder Apps Are Being Launched for Britain's Independent Female Muslims', *Vice*, 2015.

Aisha Mirza, 'Staying Alive Through Brexit', blackgirldangerous, 2016.